"Where have you been?"

"I haven't been able to reach you all day." Mike took the key from Peggy's hand, unlocked the door and ushered her into her apartment.

"When you left last night I felt empty, incomplete," Mike said.

"I always feel incomplete when I leave you, Mike," she said softly. "Always."

When she turned, Mike was standing in a corner of the living room.

"What are you doing?" Peggy asked.

"Trying to figure out how to work this thing." He was turning buttons on her record player, an ancient machine she'd picked up at a garage sale.

"Why?"

"Because tonight I missed the most beautiful woman at the ball. But I've found my Cinderella now, and I've come to claim the dance I missed."

ABOUT THE AUTHOR

Molly McGuire is the pseudonym of well-known romance writer Sally Goldenbaum. While Sally is the author of a number of romances, *My Prince Charming* is her second book for Harlequin. She has been a teacher at both the high school and college levels, as well as a textbook writer and a public-relations writer for public television. Born in Wisconsin, Sally now lives in Kansas.

Books by Molly McGuire

HARLEQUIN AMERICAN ROMANCE
436–FOREVER YOURS

MOLLY McGUIRE

MY PRINCE CHARMING

Harlequin Books

TORONTO • NEW YORK • LONDON
AMSTERDAM • PARIS • SYDNEY • HAMBURG
STOCKHOLM • ATHENS • TOKYO • MILAN
MADRID • WARSAW • BUDAPEST • AUCKLAND

To Don

Published April 1993

ISBN 0-373-16484-X

MY PRINCE CHARMING

Chapter One

Peggy Shilling breezed into Otto's Market on Columbus Avenue and grinned at the short, thin man with the wild white hair. "Otto, you need a perm," she said.

"And you need a zipper on that lip, young lady. And you also need some of my lasagna." And with that he carefully spooned a heaping portion of the casserole into a waxed cardboard box and handed it across the glass counter to her.

"Otto, you're wonderful." Peggy breathed in the wonderful smell of garlic, herbs and spicy tomato sauce. "Put it on my bill, okay?"

"You bet your boots. And what else can I do for the most ravishing beauty to grace my doorway today?"

"That's it, Otto. Your food and your corn, that's all I need to keep me going."

"Sure it is. Now get out of here, so the boy'll have some dinner."

Peggy slipped her wallet into her purse and then rushed out of the store, wondering if she'd missed her bus again. It was pulling away from the curb, attempting to merge into the busy rush hour traffic. She waved her arms frantically and raced to the curb, yelling for it to stop.

The driver finally spotted her and squealed to a halt, then opened the automatic doors and shouted at her to hurry.

Peggy swung herself into an empty seat, closed her eyes and sighed.

"Long day?" said the man next to her.

Peggy opened her eyes and looked at him sideways. Although she forced herself to be cautious about strangers, strangers on buses were different. She liked the company, and the drivers watched over her. Besides, this man looked completely harmless. So she smiled at him, settled back against the seat and said, "It was a wonderful day. Really good. I'm just tired, that's all. Did you have a nice day?"

The man took off his reading glasses and thought about that for a minute. "Did I have a nice day?" he repeated.

"Yes. You look like a man who has had a . . . well, a successful day, I guess. You're dressed so nicely. Your face is calm, you're reading the financial page of the paper without obvious stress, your tie is neat and clean—in place, not wrinkled from being tugged at and fiddled with."

Michael Kendrick was amused. "That could simply mean I've been sitting in an office all day without a thing to do."

Peggy shook her head. "No, I don't think so. You don't look like that sort of person. If you hadn't had anything to do all day you'd be a wreck, just as I would. You'd be irritable, pasty looking—"

"Pasty looking?" The man laughed.

Peggy was stopped short by his laughter. She had been talking too much, she knew that, and now she was embarrassed. But it had been such a good day. The clown troupe was finally a real part of the children's hospital routine and they were being so effective there—*really* helping those little kids. She wished she could give more than one day a week to it, but the pay was meager, and she simply couldn't afford it. But no matter, one day was better than none. She looked over at her companion and grinned. "I talk too much, don't I?" she said.

"No, not at all. I didn't mean to cut you short. I was laughing because you're charming and you say what's on your mind. It's refreshing and my guess is you're a very interesting person."

"Thank you," Peggy said, although she didn't always feel so interesting lately. But she was interested *in* things, so she supposed that made her interesting. Now this man next to her was as nice as could be, and he had a nice face, with soft laugh lines fanning out from his eyes, but he didn't look particularly interesting. Of course, she wouldn't hold that against him. Dull people had their place.

Michael was watching her carefully as she played with her thoughts. He was expert at reading people's expressions—a trait fine honed and handy in working out business deals. Now his smile broadened as he surmised some of what was going on inside her mind.

The smile caught Peggy off guard and she was briefly startled. His wasn't a polished kind of smile, but open and slightly crooked. And it didn't stop with his lips. It opened up his whole face. She knew at that moment that she'd been dead wrong; there was something in his eyes that lit up the whole bus. This man was about as dull as Nicaragua. "Aha," she said, more to herself than to the man in the suit.

At that, the man laughed again.

"I wasn't talking to you that time," she said quickly.

"Okay."

"I haven't seen you on this bus before."

"No. I don't usually ride it." He shifted, lengthening his legs under the seat in front. It was then that Peggy spotted his shoes. Her two years in the shoe department at Marshall Field's had left her tuned in to people's feet and this man's feet were walking in Cole-Haans. Expensive. She looked back to his face. "Well, it's a nice bus, friendly drivers, except when you make them stop in the middle of traffic to let you on."

He nodded. "Good."

"Tell me, just for my own curiosity, why *are* you riding this bus?"

He flashed her another smile. It was a *large* smile, as her aunt Bessie would say. No restraints.

"I'm riding this bus because I had a meeting in another part of town. I was about to call a cab when the bus pulled up. I thought, 'What the hell, Kendrick, you've never been on a bus before, go for it!' So I did."

Never been on a bus before! Peggy nodded slowly. She was right. Cole-Haans didn't ride buses.

"Normally I would have used my car," the man beside her was saying, "but it rolled down the side of a hill yesterday and landed in a lake."

Peggy looked at him sideways. She had heard lots of lines in her day, but this was a new one. Her brows drew together. She could see he was enjoying himself. "I'm sorry to hear that," she said. "About your car, I mean."

"Yeah. I was sorry, too. But those things happen sometimes. Occupational hazard."

"I suppose." She looked over at him again, still unsure about him. Many of her friends had odd senses of humor; perhaps that was what was going on here. "Occupational hazard?" she said. "What do you do?"

"Oh, different things. Yesterday I was checking on a film group connected to my company," Michael said. "We do mostly commercials and documentaries."

"About what?"

"Just about anything. Things other companies hire us to do. Some presentations for our own projects. Yesterday we happened to be shooting some film in Wisconsin at a landfill site and my beloved old car was being used as a prop when an unruly horse from a nearby field ran into it. I guess I didn't have the emergency on and it was bye-bye little Mustang."

"Maybe the horse thought it was a relative," Peggy said.

Michael laughed. "Anyway," he said, "they got it all on film and it made a great action shot. Maybe we'll find a use for it sometime."

"Sure. You never know when you'll need a car falling off a cliff." Peggy shifted in the seat, getting more comfortable and moving slightly so she had a better view of her companion's face. "You don't look much like a filmmaker," she said, taking in his clean-cut appearance. "I have a friend in film. He doesn't own a suit."

Michael glanced down at his suit, then back at Peggy. "This is what you call a sales prop. I just came from a meeting with a very prestigious group of businessmen who are interested in funding a new project of ours. The way I see it, when in Rome, do as the Romans do."

"You're right. When I was young and foolish I would have thought that a cop-out. But now I know differently. There are times when compromising is wise and necessary."

She spoke the words with such sincerity Michael got the feeling they were discussing the national debt. But then she smiled and the intensity lessened.

"Since we're sharing such profound philosophy," Michael said, "maybe we ought to pull out all stops and exchange names." He held out his hand. "I'm Michael Kendrick."

Peggy took his hand. "Hi. Peggy Shilling."

"Peggy," he repeated. Her name rolled off his tongue fluidly and Peggy suddenly felt special. It sounded like the name of royalty when he said it that way, or a movie star. Not plain old Peggy Shilling from Gary, Indiana.

"The name fits you," he said. "Peggy is a great name."

Peggy smiled, then glanced out the window. Slowly the neighborhood registered in her mind. "Oh, damn," she said, half rising. The box of lasagna slipped from her lap and hit the floor soundly. Thick red sauce splattered out onto Michael Kendrick's shiny black Cole-Haan shoes. Peggy looked down at it. "Double damn," she murmured softly.

"You missed your stop," he said.

"Yes, but not your shoes."

Michael glanced down. "It looks like good lasagna."

"It is. Was. The best in town."

"And was probably your dinner."

She nodded slowly. "I'm awfully sorry about your shoes. Here, let me help you." She bent over in the small space and tried to reach his shoes with a tissue she'd pulled from her purse.

"No need—" Michael began, but he was too late. The bus lurched to a stop and Peggy toppled over across his lap, her legs flailing out into the aisle and her head hitting the side of the bus.

Frantically she tried to right herself, but her center of balance, it seemed, was down somewhere near the lasagna.

Finally, slipping one arm beneath her body on his legs, Michael managed to help her to an upright position.

"There," he said, reluctant to let go.

Peggy clung to the seat in front of them. Tiny drops of perspiration dotted her forehead. "I'm not usually so clumsy," she mumbled.

"Wasn't your fault." He knew she was embarrassed and he would like to have eased it, but Michael couldn't concentrate. He was suddenly acutely aware of the woman whose legs pressed against his own. He had liked Peggy right off. The intelligent, bright light in her eyes was appealing, and she was great to look at. She was charming, funny, nice. And all that was fine. Lots of people were all those things. But there was something else going on here when Peggy Shilling tumbled across his legs on the Twenty-third Street bus. In that lightning-short space of time something incredibly odd happened to Michael Kendrick, bachelor of thirty-four years. He wasn't sure what it was—a shifting of particles, a moving around of atoms—but Peggy's entrance into his life was an event, the kind he urged his producers to capture on film because it would captivate audiences and maybe even change them in some way.

That was it, he decided. Somehow, in some way, this small, pretty woman with the dancing eyes was going to change his life.

Chapter Two

"Carmen, I'm here." Peggy walked into the apartment and dropped her sweater onto a chair by the door. The apartment was so tiny that announcing her arrival was more routine than necessary. Carmen and Billy were a few steps away in the square living room.

"He talked to me, Peggy!" Carmen said proudly, getting up from the sofa and walking toward Peggy with the eighteen-month-old baby in her arms.

"A genius, this one! What did he say?" Peggy took the baby from her sitter, who lived across-the-hall, and kissed the child's pink cheeks. She was entranced by him, and every time she was away from him and then came back, the enchantment grew. The feeling was always new, and the bolt of joy that shot through her was always unexpected, always unnerving. Peggy had never dreamed it was possible to love this much.

"He said, 'Camen,' of course."

"Come on, Billy," Peggy said, nuzzling the soft, sweet-smelling flesh with her nose, "talk for Mama."

Billy giggled.

"I had some wonderful lasagna for you, handsome, but it landed on a man's shoe."

"Oh, Peggy," said Carmen, slapping her cheek.

"He was a very nice man, very considerate."

Carmen was gathering up things from the couch. "Nice men are worth hanging on to. Did you?"

Peggy laughed at the memory of herself hanging off Michael Kendrick's lap. "In a manner of speaking," she said aloud.

"So when will you see him again?"

"Oh, not that kind of hanging on, Carmen. I won't see him again ev—"

The ringing of the phone cut off the end of her sentence, and Carmen automatically picked up the receiver. "Shilling residence," she said.

Billy tugged on Peggy's earring while she waited for Carmen to handle the phone call.

"It's for you, Peg," Carmen said. Her eyes sparkled.

"Who?"

"He didn't say. Just said he owed you a dinner."

Peggy frowned.

"Hey, never look a gift dinner in the mouth."

Peggy, still frowning, took the phone. "Hello?" she said tentatively. It was probably Al from the social service agency where she worked part-time. He called at least once a week on some pretense or another, although his goal was clear: to get Peggy to bed.

"Peggy, this is Michael."

"Michael?" The voice was vaguely familiar.

"Michael from the bus."

"Mike!"

His laugh was loose, deep. "That's the one," he said. "I like the inflection, by the way."

"You surprised me, that's all. How did you get my phone number?"

"Oh, I have more than that. I have your whole purse."

"Oh, damn!" Billy bounced in her arms.

"There it was, stuffed under the seat of the bus, no worse for wear, although it didn't escape the great lasagna slide."

"Well, thanks for finding it. Could you mail it to me? I'll reimburse you, of course. I don't have a car or I'd come get it."

"I'm a step ahead of you."

"You already mailed it."

"No—dinner. I ended up with your lasagna dinner. So how about if I pick you up, take you to dinner, give you your purse—"

Peggy laughed. She was being asked out! How nice, though impractical. Experience told her Billy had a way of discouraging such things very fast. "That's awfully nice of you, Mike, but I can't possibly do that. I have a baby, and . . ."

Michael paused for only a fraction of a second. "And a husband?" he asked.

"Oh, no. No husband. If I did, I could leave the baby with him." She laughed lightly.

"Well, then, that's no problem," Michael said. "We'll take the baby along."

"To dinner?"

"Sure. What does he like?"

"Mike, he's eighteen months old."

"Steak is out, huh?"

"I think so." She was smiling in spite of herself. The man had a definite flair.

"Well, we'll think of something. Maybe Italian, I guess, since he lost out on the lasagna, or Chinese. That can be easily gummed if he doesn't have a lot of teeth."

Now Peggy was laughing out loud.

"Are you doubting my sincerity?"

"No, no. But I don't even know you."

"Oh, come on, Peggy. That sounds like a bad soap. One short bus ride with you told me you aren't the bad soap type."

"Mike, I have to go. Billy is chewing on my ear."

"Mmm. That's a nice thought."

"Please mail me my purse?"

"No."

"No?"

"No. You get it back only with strings attached. Sorry, but that's the way it is. And the strings include dinner. You, me and Billy. No compromises. That's it."

"And you're paying?"

"Yes."

Peggy paused for just a minute before she agreed. The man was a bit daft, but he had a nice face, and good lord, how many men would attack a woman with a baby in her lap?

She dressed Billy in the only clothes that were clean—tiny jeans and a red checked shirt. He looked like a cowboy. And as for herself, she showered off the lasagna that had splattered onto her body, then

quickly pulled on a bright blue knit dress. Thank
heavens, she thought, for her friend Casey's castoffs.

Mike was prompt. At 6:57 the buzzer rang. At 7:00
he stood just outside her door.

All Peggy's misgivings about having dinner with the
man disappeared as soon as she opened the door. He
stood there in neatly pressed slacks and a navy blue
sports jacket. Clutched in one hand was a bouquet of
red-and-blue balloons, and beneath his arm was an
enormous plastic worm with bright blue wheels. Peggy's purse dangled from three fingers.

"Mike!" she said. Behind her Billy squealed and
clapped his hands.

Michael smiled at her, then walked past her and over
to the playpen where Billy was grasping the rail, his
huge eyes following every one of Michael's movements. "You must be the man of the house," Michael said. "How do you do?"

Billy grinned.

Peggy stood a step behind Michael. "Where did you
get those things?"

"I have my sources," he said, and set the plastic
riding toy and her purse down on the floor. The balloons escaped his grasp and headed up to the tall ceiling.

"They're perfect."

"I was that age once myself, you know."

"Of course."

And then Peggy found herself, for perhaps the first
time in her life, at a loss for words. She simply stood
and stared at him. What she wanted to do was out of

the question; devouring him with her eyes would have to suffice.

"Well, Peggy and Billy, are you going to make me stand here all night? Or can we get the show on the road?"

Michael carried Billy, and Peggy locked the double locks on her door and followed him down the narrow stairway and out to the street. Peggy stepped over a heap of litter that had fallen out of a trash can. "It's usually easier to get a cab down on the corner," she said and began walking in that direction.

"I have a car," Michael said.

"But the Mustang—"

"I borrowed a car."

It was then that Peggy's eyes adjusted to the deepening twilight. The narrow street in front of her apartment was always lined with cars. Most of them she recognized, but the one parked directly in the middle of the street—because it would never in a million years fit into a parking spot—she definitely didn't. She looked up at Michael, her eyes wide. "No, Mike..."

"I apologize, Peggy. I know it seems pretentious as hell but it was all I could get my hands on."

Peggy slowly took her eyes off Mike's face and looked back at the car. "A limo? My lord, who *are* you—"

"I told you, it's not mine, but I didn't think it would be convenient to take the bus or a cab with Billy, and this is all I could get on short notice. But if you have strong objections to it, I'll call a cab."

"And you'll leave it here? The neighborhood kids would love you. They could make enough on the hubcaps alone to retire for a couple of months."

Michael looked at the squirming baby in his arms. "Billy, it might be just you and me tonight. She's being difficult. Maybe we could take in a Cubs game and then—"

"Let's go." Peggy grabbed his elbow, and at that moment a uniformed chauffeur stepped out of the car and without a word opened the back door.

"Thank you," Peggy said quietly and slipped into the richly smelling leather interior of the grand vehicle. Mike was right behind her. In minutes he had Billy strapped into a car seat opposite Peggy, and he sat beside it. Store tags dangling from the side of it brushed against his leg.

Peggy shook her head. This must be some sort of a dream. When she'd tripped in the bus she had hit her head and she was probably still there, on the floor of the bus, dreaming these outrageous, incredible dreams.

"Billy, what are we doing here?" she said to the smiling baby.

"Ca-men," Billy answered.

"What?"

Billy said it again, and while Michael watched, huge tears welled up in Peggy's eyes. In seconds they were falling unchecked down her cheeks.

"Peggy, what's wrong?" he asked. He leaned forward and took her hands in his, but the movement only seemed to fuel the tears, and as the car moved slowly down the narrow street, Peggy, her eyes focused on the beautiful baby boy in front of her, cried profusely. Michael grabbed some tissue from the cabinet and handed her a fistful.

"Thanks," she managed between intakes of breath, and then, as quickly as they had begun, the tears stopped. "I'm so sorry, Mike," she said. She took another tissue and blew her nose.

"That's okay. This happens all the time."

Peggy managed a smile.

"Can I help?"

"No. It's Billy. It . . . it was his first word."

Michael nodded as if he understood.

"He . . . he said Carmen."

"Beautiful opera. Billy has good taste."

"No, it's the girl who takes care of him."

Again, Michael nodded. He had had no experience with kids or with babies. He *thought* he understood women—he had had a lot of experience with them. Obviously he was wrong. "Peggy, I'm not sure if you're happy or sad about this."

"Oh, happy! I'm so happy—" And then the tears came again.

"Well, good! We have cause for celebration, right, big boy?" He winked at Billy, then pulled open the bottom section of the teak cabinet and pulled out a bottle of champagne. "It just so happens we're always prepared for first words." Michael deftly uncorked the bottle and poured the champagne into two crystal glasses. He handed one to Peggy and softly clinked the edge of his glass to hers. "Here's to first words."

"To first words," Peggy repeated, and took a large swallow of champagne. It slid down her throat as easily as apple juice, as though she drank it every day. And then, with a vengeance, it hit her empty stomach and she felt a heady rush. "Mike," she said finally, "just exactly who are you?"

"We covered all that on the bus. We should be well on our way to more interesting things."

Peggy was not deterred. "Whose car is this?"

"My father's."

Peggy was silent.

"I needed a car, as I told you—"

"Because yours fell down a hill."

"Right. And the company's cars were all tied up. So I called my father's office, and this is what they sent over."

"I see."

"And this is the restaurant, so let's go. Billy's hungry."

Peggy looked down at her son, who was gnawing delightedly on the end of the seat strap. "Okay. I think I need some firm land beneath my feet."

But once out of the car the earth began to sway more violently.

Peggy stared ahead. Mike knew she had an eighteen-month-old baby. She had expected a McDonald's or maybe a Howard Johnson. Some kind of family place with hamburgers and spaghetti. Instead, looming large and elegant against the night sky was Evenings, a blue-awninged restaurant set in a palatial building with three uniformed doormen. The awning spanned the entrance, and beneath it was a wide strip of thick, matching carpet that stretched all the way to the curb.

"Oh, Mike, I don't know...." she said.

"It's a great restaurant, Peggy. You'll love it."

"But the baby—"

"He'll love it, too. Trust me."

Her choices being limited, she held tight to the banana she had brought for Billy and followed Mike inside. And there, inside the beveled-glass doors, she was assaulted with an elegance that made her head swim. The carpets were so thick she nearly lost her balance, and the fabric-covered walls, the gold-edged mirrors and the tuxedoed string quartet playing in the distance did nothing at all to steady her.

Beneath a stretch of floor-to-ceiling windows the choppy waters of Lake Michigan, softly lit by hidden spotlights, lapped against the shore.

Peggy looked up at Michael and shook her head slowly.

"You don't like it?"

"Mike—" she realized she was whispering but she couldn't stop herself "—Mike, this isn't what you would call a family restaurant."

"I come here with my family all the time."

"A *baby* family restaurant. Mike, they won't be able to handle Billy."

"You're a real worrywart, Peggy. What's to handle?" Mike looked down at Billy, whose chubby arms were wound tightly around his neck.

Just then a distinguished gray-haired man approached them and greeted Mike with a deference Peggy thought only afforded to the clergy.

"There are two of you tonight, Mr. Kendrick?" he asked in mellow, well-modulated tones, his thin brows lifting up into his receding hairline.

Michael laughed. "The boy's well behaved, but he's real, just the same," he said, nodding toward Billy. "There are *three* of us, Simon, and from the way this kid is chewing on my collar, he's the hungriest of all."

"I see," said Simon. He frowned.

"What does he need, Peggy?" Michael asked. "Phone books?"

"He needs a high chair, Mike," she said, still in hushed, library tones.

"A high chair," Simon repeated, still frowning.

Peggy suppressed a smile. Coming from Simon's lips, the words sounded foreign.

"Yes," said Mike. "Billy needs a high chair, Simon."

"A high chair." Simon's brow furrowed so deeply Peggy was sure it would never smooth out again. "Certainly, Mr. Kendrick," he finally said. "It will be only a moment." He looked around then and clicked two fingers, which sent a flurry of uniformed young men into orbit.

Peggy watched Mike. He was oblivious to it all, and had absolutely no idea that this restaurant had never before had a toddler in its midst. She shook her head, then decided it was his world and he could handle it. So when Mike cupped her elbow and nodded toward a retreating maître d', she followed silently. The table to which he led them was in a smaller room with large curved windows that framed the lake beyond. Damask floor-length tablecloths cushioned the most beautiful blue-and-gold-edged china that Peggy had ever seen.

"Billy's not used to such elegance," Peggy said finally. She held him tightly in her lap.

"You're going to choke him, Peggy," Mike said.

"I don't want him to break anything."

"Hey, relax! This is his treat, too, right, old man?"

At that moment several waiters appeared. Two of them carried an ornately carved high chair that looked like something stolen from the Smithsonian Institution. "Will this be suitable, Mr. Kendrick?" the maître d' asked.

Mike looked at Peggy, who was busy calculating how long it would take her to pay for any damage done to the elaborate, collector's chair.

"Peggy?" Mike prompted. "Do you think this is okay?"

She nodded numbly and watched as Mike picked Billy up and slipped him into the chair. His short, square feet thumped happily against the wooden foot ledge.

"Perfect," Mike said and sat down again. "I knew Billy would like this place."

Peggy simply sighed and stuck a bread stick into the baby's fist.

The sommelier, who called Mike "Mr. Kendrick" in a tone of such respect Peggy found herself nodding her head each time he said the words, appeared with a bottle of champagne. He turned the label to Mike, who nodded, and then the man poured an inch into Mike's glass for his approval. Peggy watched in amazement as a pâté was placed on the table, along with delicate toast points and a plate holding strips of meat covered with a lemony sauce that Michael called carpaccio.

"Mike, can they read your mind? The waiters, I mean."

"I hope not," he said, and the smile he gave Peggy sent ripples of pleasure racing up her arms and legs.

"Mr. Kendrick," a new waiter said at Mike's elbow, "the cook shall prepare a lovely scallop dish for you and the lady—his own recipe—and something perhaps less gourmet for the baby."

"Thanks, Henry, that sounds great."

Peggy watched the waiter disappear. He made absolutely no sound while he walked, and Peggy wondered if his feet touched the floor.

"Do you like it here, Bill?" Mike asked, directing his attention to the toddler in the high chair.

The little boy picked up a spoon and banged it on the wooden high-chair tray in response. Peggy grimaced.

"Good. Thought you would," Mike said. He turned his attention back to Peggy. "And the lady?"

"The lady is snowed. I think I'm dreaming. I mean, can you imagine how I feel, Mike? I don't even know you. You're a white knight who dropped out of nowhere and whisked me and my child off to the palace—one, by the way, that probably has *never* opened its doors to kids before. I'm sure that high chair is from someone's antique collection!"

"I've always thought antiques should be used."

"Well, this one will be well used, I'm afraid, by the time Billy gets out of it."

"If you're uncomfortable, Peggy..."

"Out of place, Mike, not uncomfortable."

Mike looked around the room, glanced at the string quartet, at two elderly patrons at a nearby table, at the stack of silverware and delicate cups and saltshakers that Peggy had removed from Billy's range. And then he began to laugh, a slow, deep rumble that made Billy stop chewing on the gold napkin ring and made Peggy smile.

"How do you know I don't do this every night?" he asked at last. "Who are you to say I don't ride buses all day, looking for unsuspecting young mothers that I can bring here and—"

Now Peggy was laughing, as well. "Okay, maybe you do, Mike Kendrick. Who am I to doubt it? But believe it or not, I don't do this every day."

"Well, good," Mike said simply. "Now promise me one thing or I'm going to whisk you both right out of here."

"What?"

"Promise me you'll trust me enough to relax and enjoy the evening. If Billy breaks anything they won't even blink. My family has spent enough money here to make an antique high chair or a flowered cup seem rather insignificant, so please don't let it wrinkle that beautiful forehead of yours. It's not worth it." He stopped talking and his eyes focused on her with such intensity that Peggy coughed beneath his look.

"Is that a promise?" he asked.

Peggy took a quick drink of champagne and smiled. "Yes."

"Good. Let's eat." And as if by magic a waiter appeared with the first course, a delicate green salad with smooth hearts of palm in the center.

"Tell me one thing, Mike," Peggy said when the waiter had left. "I'm all relaxed—I promise—but *why* did you do this?"

"You mean having dinner with you, I guess."

"Yes, exactly! It's lovely and all that, but I can't for the life of me figure out why a man like you would do this. Do you . . . do you do this sort of thing often?"

"Well, do you?"

"Do I what?" Peggy asked.

He was smiling at her now, an enigmatic, handsome smile that made Peggy shift in her chair.

"Do you go out to dinner with strange men you've met on buses often," he said patiently.

"Never."

"Good. It isn't safe, and for the record, this is a first for me. You are my one and only bus pickup."

Peggy grinned. "Well, that's good."

"Now that we've settled that and I know I'm safe with you, tell me some more about Peggy Shilling. And about Billy."

Peggy eyed the crystal cup of cold, spicy shrimp that was put before her. She handed a shrimp to Billy and then looked up at Mike. "There's not much to tell. You know where I live, you've met Billy, I told you about my job when we were on the bus—"

"No, you didn't. I told you about me, and you were polite and interested, but you didn't tell me anything about you."

"Oh. Well, okay. I do this and that."

Mike laughed again. She did it so easily, caused this ripple of pleasure to coast along his insides. It was terrific, better than ten-year-old Scotch after a twenty-hour day. And utterly crazy, considering she was the mother of this small, charming kid, who must have, somewhere along the way, had a father. "Okay, Peggy," he said. "Could you expand a little?"

"A little. I work part-time for a social service agency. There's not a lot of money right now so I never know how much work they'll have. I do some publicity, press releases, and I help arrange some fund-raisers, that sort of thing."

"What kind of fund-raisers?" Since he had first met Peggy, Mike had been impressed with the fact that she didn't remind him of anyone he knew; she was completely different from the women who peopled his social world. But fund-raisers were something close to home. Nearly every woman with whom he'd ever been associated ran some sort of gala fund-raiser for whatever was the latest cause. He had been to more charity balls and celebrity auctions than he wanted to remember, and he had a brief sensation of wanting to stop Peggy, to hold back the words so he could keep her separate from all that.

"What's the matter, Mike?" Peggy was leaning forward, her elbows resting slightly on the table, her face concerned.

He forced a smile. "Nothing. Go on. What kind of fund-raisers?"

"Well, the fund-raisers we do are kind of fun. Last Friday we had an all-day hamburger bash at Elmo's Burgers down near the loop. Every year Elmo sets aside one day, sells the burgers for thirty cents each and gives us his entire take for the day. Can you believe it? The *whole* thing. It's great. We all take shifts, pitch in and flip burgers. My hair smells like grease for weeks afterward, my feet swell, but we make a ton of money.''

Mike felt a cool, fresh breeze blow through his head. He smiled. "How much?"

"This year we broke a record." She smiled, a giant smile that lifted her whole face. "Two thousand dollars," she said.

Her pride was infectious and he smiled back. The fact was that the fund-raisers he knew about involved far more than that spent just on postage, but that all suddenly seemed insignificant. "That's great, Peggy," he said. "What's the money used for?"

"A million things. We donate to a shelter for battered women, a halfway house for kids—" She glanced over at Billy, then lowered her voice and said, "That's where I found Billy. Left in a basket at our door, just like Moses."

"You're not his mother?" The words jumped out, carried on a current of approval.

"Of course I'm his mother. Now." She frowned and her voice softened. "I'm his mother—"

Mike smiled at her, a soothing, apologetic kind of smile. "Sorry, Peggy. Of course you're his mother. He loves the devil out of you, that's as plain as the banana on his nose."

Peggy smiled and dabbed at the yellow glop Billy had pressed on his face.

"So you adopted him, you're saying?"

She nodded and handed Billy another shrimp. "It took every ounce of courage in me. Bureaucracies are damned hard to fight. They don't like to give babies to single women, of course. And I understand it on one hand, but on the other, I'm sure a better alternative than an institution!" Her face was flushed now and Mike noticed there were sparks of fire flashing in her green eyes. He leaned forward, not wanting to miss a word, wanting her to go on talking.

And then she stopped, let the words drop off, and she leaned over to Billy and kissed him on his cheek. When she looked up at Mike her eyes were moist but her voice was strong. "But it was worth every bit of it," she said. "Don't you think?"

He didn't know if it was worth it. Michael Kendrick liked kids—Billy seemed great as kids go—but he knew little about them, except that they were raised by nannies, not beautiful young women. He looked at the baby and then back to Peggy and he thought of all the women he knew who had prevented pregnancies, some for such simple reasons as to avoid the inconvenience.

But Peggy's face, beaming as she kissed the fat cheek of her son, refused to let him think of any of that. The look on her face said that yes, having Billy was worth nearly anything in the world. He nodded. "You're crazy about him, that's clear."

"I've had Billy since he was a couple of weeks old, but the adoption was only final last month. The agency did some investigative work and found out his mother overdosed after she left him with us. The father was never known."

Mike couldn't speak for a minute. A young woman taking on the life of a child born of a drug addict. "Have you—" he started.

"Oh, sure," Peggy said. "I had Billy checked over completely, and thank goodness there was no trace of drugs in him. His biological mother must have stayed off just long enough for Billy to be born, probably the greatest gift she ever gave anyone. She must have at least loved him enough to do that."

Mike watched her closely, and while she talked about Billy her eyes filled with tears. She brushed them away unselfconsciously, then leaned over and kissed Billy. Mike knew she probably did that frequently. Love seemed to flow out of Peggy Shilling in rivers. "Remarkable," he said softly.

"Billy?" Peggy said, her eyes still shining. "Yes, he's my miracle."

"No," Mike said. "I meant you."

Peggy lowered her head to hide the pleasure with which his words filled her, and then the waiter came and rescued her from the moment. The uniformed young man filled their table with new gold-rimmed plates, this time holding scallops in a delicate wine sauce, thin strands of pasta and crisp vegetables. Peggy felt her head spin from all the sensual delights; first there was Mike, who made her swell inside until she had to squirm in her chair, and then there were the sensory delights of the food. And Billy was right beside her, happily chewing narrow strips of chicken that she knew tasted nothing like the food he was used to. Cinderella, she thought. She glanced at her watch.

And it was nearly time for the pumpkin to reappear.

Dinner was over in what seemed to Peggy to be a flash of dreamy light, but not before Mike beckoned to the string quartet from their small carpeted niche to play an improvised version of "Oh, Where Have You Been, Billy Boy?" for her son.

And then they were off into the crisp Chicago night, gliding through the streets in the sumptuous limo and arriving at Peggy's apartment with a sleeping bundle of boy slumped comfortably forward in the brand-new car seat.

With Peggy's help Mike undid the straps and buckles, carefully lifted Billy from the car seat and carried him up the three flights of stairs to Peggy's apartment.

"Mike," she said after fumbling with the key, "I don't know how to thank you for this."

A thin shaft of light from the open door of her apartment fell across her hair. Mike wanted to touch it, to smooth the reddish lock back over her forehead. Instead he spoke around the lump in his throat.

"No thanks necessary," he said. "It was a business deal." His heart was pounding inside his chest like a young kid's. What was this woman, a witch? He thought if she moved one inch closer to him he'd be over the edge, not a great place to be with an eighteen-month-old baby in his arms.

"I'll take Billy," Peggy said.

"Oh, sure." The sleeping baby quickly changed hands. The cool rush of air steadied Mike's thoughts slightly. He smiled. "I think he needs a diaper change."

"You're learning, Mike," she said.

They stood for a moment in silence. Outside, the traffic was a late-night sound, with a siren falling off in the distance. Peggy shifted Billy from one hip to the other.

Finally she met Mike's eyes and spoke. "Mike, there's one more thing." She leaned forward so he could hear her without disturbing the baby. Her voice was low and husky.

Automatically Mike bent toward her. He felt a tightening in his groin.

"About your shoes, Mike." Her eyes were huge, her brows lifted up into her thick auburn hair. "Don't...don't use water to get the lasagna off. Leather cleaner...use leather cleaner."

And then, before he had a chance to straighten up or process her words, she had disappeared inside the small apartment and a cold wind, leaking into the narrow hallway from a cracked window at the other end, was all that brushed past Michael Kendrick's lips.

Chapter Three

Three weeks passed, and each day Peggy thought perhaps Mike Kendrick would call. Each night she convinced herself those were foolish thoughts. When Mike had returned her and Billy safely to their apartment that night he had said nothing about seeing them again. He had been polite and gracious. But then he had left, and from her third-floor window she had watched him climb into the limo and be driven down the narrow street. It was a fluke, she told herself, a happenstance, and Mike Kendrick was a nice man who wanted to make up for the dinner she had dumped on the bus floor. Nothing more than that, surely.

Her life would go on as always, and she'd have that nice, happy memory of a night on the town with the dark-haired stranger to pull out on long winter nights. And that was that. Peggy took a deep breath, adjusted the brown grocery sack in her arms and pushed open the door of her apartment.

"Mama," Billy said when she walked through the door. Peggy's heart soared, pushing all other thoughts into the shadow of her mind.

"Billy boy," she said back, scooping the toddler into her arms.

And then she looked up and instead of Carmen, Mike Kendrick sat in her direct line of vision, his long legs spread nearly halfway across the room. "Hi, Peggy," he said.

His fingers were tented beneath his chin, his head slightly lowered, and he looked up at her through dark blue eyes that took her breath away. He wore jeans and tennis shoes today, and a knit polo shirt that stretched across his chest. But it didn't matter. He looked the same—elegant and sexy and . . . and out of place.

"Hi, Mike," she said, trying very hard to be calm and to disguise the fact that in the three weeks she'd had to think about him he had become as familiar to her as her own breathing.

"I got back in town this week and came over to see if Billy had learned any more words."

"Dozens," she said, setting the wiggling boy down. "He's another Einstein. Once the connection was made, the words poured out."

"Is he writing tomes yet?"

Peggy laughed. "Next week."

"He's bigger." Mike looked at Billy, who was pulling a small three-wheeled plastic bike through the door.

"They do that," Peggy said.

"I was out of town," Mike said again, as if he owed her an explanation. He didn't, he knew. In fact, he had realized once he was away from Peggy that whatever attraction he felt for her didn't make a lot of sense. Mike didn't believe much in the strictures class put on one, but he knew instinctively that Peggy Shilling would shun the kind of things that inevitably crept into his world. It wasn't until Joe Paling, the head of the studio, told him about the snags in the new documentary, that seeing Peggy became a rational option.

"Were you on vacation?" Peggy asked him now.

"Wedding," Michael said. "A family friend, not mine."

Peggy smiled. "Oh. Well, that's nice."

"Yes."

Billy tripped over Mike's legs then, and Michael lifted him up. Peggy noticed how huge his hands were as they supported the small boy. Large, expressive hands.

"I guess I shouldn't have come by unannounced like this," Mike was saying, "but I was nearby and there was something I wanted to talk to you about, so I thought I would chance your being home."

"Oh?" Peggy flopped down in the chair across from him. *So talk, Mike,* her mind was saying. *Say anything you want, anything that will keep you sitting in front of me for a while.*

"Our film company is doing this documentary on abused women. We need to get a few people on board who know something about the field and can help direct the slant of the film. When we were talking the other night, you mentioned the place you did some work for had a connection in that area and I thought we might be able to use your expertise. You could be kind of a liaison for us."

"Oh, you mean the Family Haven Center. It's a wonderful place. Sure, what do you want to know?"

"Well, lots of things. If you're interested, we can talk more with some of my people and work out a consultant's fee."

"Don't be silly. I'll tell you anything you want to know. Forget about the consultant bit. I'd just like people to know more about the center."

"Can't do that, it messes up the funding. This documentary is tied to a grant. We need to hire you in order for it to work out all right on paper."

"You know, that's why the economy is in such a mess, because of that kind of thinking!"

Mike laughed. "And your attitude, Miss Shilling, is why the money often ends up in the wrong pockets. Take what is owed you."

Peggy grinned. "Since you put it like that..." She looked down at Billy. There was always a place to use money, that was for sure. Just this morning she was wondering how to scrounge up the three weeks' babysitting money she owed Carmen. She looked back at Mike. "I'd be glad to help. I'm only part-time at the social service agency right now—they had a cutback in funds—so I do have some extra time on my hands."

Mike got up out of the chair. "Great. When can you come down to the office?"

"I can juggle my hours, so you name it."

They settled on the next day, and after Mike left, Peggy lifted Billy into her arms and danced around the small room. "Billy, my boy," she said, her voice lilting like a fine Irish song, "there is a silver lining to everything. I may even be able to pay my rent this month.''

Billy clapped his chubby hands delightedly.

PEGGY STOOD on the sidewalk and looked up at the glass-fronted building. The top of it, she was sure, was surrounded by clouds. The building was just off Michigan Avenue in a posh area of Chicago, a section of the city Peggy rarely saw. She frowned, wondering if this was such a hotshot idea. She had had to leave Billy at a neighbor's house because Carmen had a class at the university, and it was going to cost her an arm and a leg. On the other hand, maybe this job would help solve some of those money problems. Well, she'd go on up and see what they were talking about, that's what she'd do. And then she'd make a decision. With renewed purpose she headed toward the large wide doors, her shoulder bag sailing through the air.

The sound she heard was muted at first, a *whoop* kind of noise. But the sound that followed was easier to decipher.

"Damn it to hell, young woman!" a stern, angry voice intoned. "Exactly what in tarnation do you think you are doing?"

Peggy stopped in her tracks. The gray-haired man speaking to her was holding a flattened cigar in one hand. With the other he was angrily brushing ashes off his suit. More ashes were scattered on the ground and a black patch of them was flattened on the back of her purse.

"You damn near set me on fire," the man muttered as he brushed ashes off his expensive suit.

"I'm terribly sorry—"

"I ought to sue you!" The man's whole face was red now. "Damn fool woman!" He scowled at her, then flung the remains of his cigar onto the sidewalk and stalked down the street.

Peggy, shaken, stared after him. He was impeccably dressed and not a single strand of his combed gray hair was out of place. His walk was firm, angry, decisive. She shivered. Then she looked down at her purse and moaned softly. There was a large hole with angry charred edges on the back of it. Not only did the burn look awful, it was the only decent bag she had! But it was too late to worry about it now. She had ten minutes to reach the eighteenth floor of the glass building, and with the luck she was having, the elevator would probably get stuck.

She turned her purse around, pressed it to her side and walked resolutely toward the wide doors.

The cool marble lobby drew her inside and she strode with forced confidence over to the directory, her eyes quickly scanning the list of the building's occupants. With the exception of a French restaurant, a bank and a few investment firms, the building was devoted to Kendrick Enterprises. The eighteenth floor, she discovered, held the executive office suites.

"Good lord," she murmured out loud. A man in a three-piece suit smiled indulgently at her, then stepped aside to allow her onto the elevator.

"OKAY, MICHAEL, exactly who is Peggy what's her name and why the hell are we waiting for her?"

"I explained who she is, Joe. Calm down. She'll be here any minute."

"You know what I think of consultants? *Everybody*'s a consultant these days. Everyone thinks he's an expert and none of them know anything."

"Peggy's different. Trust me." Mike leaned back in the high-backed leather chair. The truth was he had no idea whether or not she'd show up, but he hoped so. He also didn't know if she knew a lot. What he *did* know was that she needed the money, so he'd gone out on a limb and trusted not only that she'd come, but that she'd have something to offer.

A middle-aged woman appeared in the doorway. "Mr. Kendrick," she said respectfully, "a Ms. Shilling is here to see you."

Michael nodded toward his secretary, then sat forward and looked over at Joe Paling. His brows lifted in an I-told-you-so gesture.

"We'll see, Kendrick," Joe muttered as he walked over to a mirrored bar and poured himself another cup of coffee.

Joe was not only a close friend of Mike's since adolescence and then onto Harvard—class of '81—but a brilliant filmmaker, as well, and he was one of the few employees of Kendrick Enterprises who didn't stand in awe of Michael and his father. Joe always said exactly what was on his mind and Michael Kendrick, even when he didn't agree, always listened.

"Hi, Mike," Peggy said, rushing into the room. "I'm sorry I'm late but the day turned into a major, muddled mess. Billy cried buckets when I left him, and I missed the el, then had to—" She noticed the other man then and her words dropped off. She lifted her head up, stood taller and tried to regain her composure. "Oh," she said, "I'm sorry. I didn't know anyone else was here."

Michael stood and walked around the desk. Of course she had come. He knew she would. "Hi, Peggy," he said warmly, then cupped her elbow and led her over to the oval table where Joe was now standing. "Peggy Shilling, I'd like you to meet Joseph Paling—"

"*The* Joseph Paling?" Peggy said. Her brows shot up into a thick wave of russet hair that swept across her forehead. "You made that documentary on the Indiana factories that won the film award."

"Now how the hell do you know that?" Joe asked, trying unsuccessfully to mask his pleasure. "It was a nice award but hasn't exactly made me a household word."

"Well, it certainly should have. It was a very fine piece of work. And you were the first one with the guts to touch those mills and the terrible conditions in them. It was long overdue."

"Well, thank you, ma'am. It was actually a collective idea—Michael here had some input. But of course," he added with a smile, "the brilliance was mine."

Mike watched the interchange and a slow smile crossed his face. For some damnable reason he had wanted these two people to get along. He wanted them to like each other, not *too* much, but enough to be friends.

"And what makes you so smug, Kendrick?" Joe said.

"Nothing. I like being right, that's all."

Joe laughed, but Peggy stood back and eyed the two men. "Am I missing something?"

"No," Joe said. "It's simply that I always question Mike's judgment. I consider it part of my job here. He said I'd like working with you, and he was right, I suspect."

"Well, I'm not sure work is the right word. Mike said you might like some input on the Family Haven project, and I'm more than willing to give it because I think it's a terrific place. We need more places like that."

"That's what I need, a believer, as well as someone who knows the ropes. Sometimes access is hard."

"That's because it's important to keep some of the things—the location, for example—as secret as possible. It helps protect the women, and many of them need that kind of protection, not just from their offenders, but from curiosity seekers."

Her eyes were flashing now, brilliant shades of green flecked with gold. Michael watched in silent appreciation as she and Joe talked on about the project. She was certainly unusual, this one. He had given jobs to people before on whims, and they usually turned out okay, but this situation was different. Peggy Shilling wasn't anything like anyone he had ever met before, and he wondered briefly, with a kind of alarming intuition, if it was a mistake to hire her.

And then, as he looked at her again, she laughed at something Joe said, that sparkling, lifting laughter that made him think of silent snowfalls on bright, crisp days, and he brushed aside the feeling. It was a ridiculous thought. Peggy was bright, refreshing and, he was beginning to think, quite beautiful, but she wasn't dangerous.

"So, Joe, what kind of a schedule can you work out with Peggy?" he said now.

"Whatever Peggy wants."

"What luxury!" Peggy said. She laughed again, shifting her purse on her hip. With the movement, a thin trickle of coins—nickels and dimes and several bus tokens—fell from her bag to the thick carpet. A hairbrush followed the coins, and before Peggy could stop it, a well-used pacifier and an empty baby bottle thudded unceremoniously to the floor.

Mike and Joe watched the stream of objects settle onto the carpet. Then they both looked at Peggy.

She shrugged, a half smile on her face. "It was bigger than I thought."

The men looked confused.

"The hole," she explained, turning her purse around. On the back near the bottom was a charred hole the size of an orange. The odor of burned leather wafted up when she moved her purse.

"Is your purse on fire?" Mike asked.

"Not anymore," Peggy said calmly. "Now, gentlemen, we better talk business because I have exactly thirty minutes before I need to catch the El."

BUT IT WAS AN HOUR and a half before Peggy left, and then, at Mike's insistence, it was in a company limo, chauffeured by a man named Larry who never spoke but whose flat gray eyes, focused on the rearview mirror, glanced her way at every stop sign.

She had resisted Mike's offer to pay for the babysitter, as well as his suggestion they get something to eat and discuss any details she might not be clear on. Things were crowding in on her, unreal things that made her feel a little as if she was in a surreal world where things had no grounding. She squeezed her eyes shut, then opened them again. Everything was still there—the glass window separating her from Larry, the nice-smelling leather seats, the teak bar. She leaned her head back and grinned. Oh, what the heck, she might as well enjoy it while it lasted. If it was a mirage or a crazy mistake or a dream, it would disappear soon enough.

Joe Paling was a nice fellow, she thought. He'd be easy to work with and she felt safe around him. It was a feeling she definitely didn't have around Michael Kendrick.

She looked out the tinted windows and watched the elegance of Michigan Avenue give way to crowded buildings as the luxurious car headed northwest toward her apartment, and as she looked she thought about this newest turn in her life.

Things never happened in ordinary ways for Peggy Shilling. They came in unplanned, unpredictable ways, like the customer in the deli renting her an apartment, or Billy being left on the doorstep at the agency, and the lasagna falling on Mike Kendrick's foot. Lasagna, of all things. And she wasn't even Italian. She shook her head. Her life wasn't simple, true, but she wouldn't trade it.

She thought back to Kendrick Enterprises, to Mike and Joe and a part-time job that would pay the rent and then some. Tomorrow she would meet the rest of the crew, Joe had said. And then they'd do some brainstorming on new approaches to take on the film.

It was all very exciting to her, even if she was only on the fringes. She knew little about filmmaking, but Joe had assured her that was fine, maybe even preferable. He didn't need another person telling him how to make films. What he needed was an idea person.

An idea person. Peggy smiled at the thought of it. She had always been told she was a doer, but now someone was actually going to pay attention to what came out of her head. Nice. She thought of her skeptical friend Casey Hendricks, who had called the night before. When told about her consultant job she'd laughed and said, "Peg, do they know what they're dealing with here? Do they realize that the only way you can think about anything is by carrying a placard or writing to the mayor, or jumping in headfirst and insisting that justice reign?"

She laughed now, remembering the conversation. Okay, so sometimes she was outspoken. She'd behave this time. She'd watch her *p*'s and *q*'s and remind herself frequently that this wasn't a job requiring her political opinion. The salary that Kendrick Enterprises was offering her for this project was enormous, many times what she made at her other job. So she'd behave, that's all.

And then she'd buy Billy new shoes.

The phone was ringing when she walked into her apartment.

"Well?" It was Casey, calling from the courthouse where she was an assistant D.A. "Give me the scoop, Pegs."

"I got the job, Casey. They want me. They want my *mind*."

"Well, it's about time. For all your heart, Peggy, you're one of the brightest friends I have. And you could do far worse than work for the Kendricks. We're talking major power here."

"So you said."

"I have met Michael, you know."

"You have? When?" Peggy's voice lifted.

"At a seminar last year. A group of civic leaders— all the heavies—were invited and Michael Kendrick was there with his father, representing the dynasty. It's so big I guess they needed two representatives."

"What's his father like?"

"Oh, my, the father. Well, Richard Joseph Kendrick the fourth is quite a man, the kind that can cause your legs to turn to Jell-O with a single, awful look. A real power mogul."

"Mike isn't that way."

"No, I hear he's a nice guy. The most eligible bachelor around. But they say he has the old man's drive, Peggy, so be careful."

"Be careful of what? I'm only there to do a part-time job and collect a walloping paycheck." Billy squirmed out of her arms and teetered across the room. "Do you know what they offer consultants these days, Casey?"

Casey moaned. "Don't tell me," she said. "The fair city of Chicago isn't nearly as kind to its overworked employees, I'm afraid."

"Well, the Kendrick outfit pays enough that I can finally take you to dinner and repay some of the dozens of meals you've given me and Billy."

"I'd prefer you forget about dinners and move out of that neighborhood. But anyway, I have to go. Justice calls. . . ."

By the time Peggy hung up the phone and found Billy, he was leaning over the toilet seat, happily dropping Peggy's small collection of lipsticks and blush powders into the water and watching them disappear down the hole.

"Oh, Billy boy," she said, and she scooped him up, nuzzling his soft neck and breathing in the calming baby smell of him.

HOURS LATER, when Billy was finally down and night shadows had lengthened across the tiny living room, Peggy slipped off her shoes and curled up on the couch. Before her, spread out in neat rows, were the information sheets Joe Paling had given her on the film project. There were also some sheets dealing with her temporary employment and a brochure on the Kendrick company's policies.

There was a brief history of the company, and a short bio on each of the principals. Peggy read it intently. Mike had two sisters, she discovered, and Kendrick Enterprises owned a good portion of Cook County. The company was enormous in its reach, far beyond anything she could ever have imagined, including in its hold newspapers, hotels, shopping centers, as well as the film company and several other small enterprises.

Finally she shoved the papers aside and rested her head on the back of the worn couch. Her hands fell limp in her lap. When she closed her eyes she tried to think ahead, to put plans in place: baby-sitters, bus routes, clean clothes, grocery shopping and her job with the SMILE group. For two years Peggy had been active in the clown troupe that visited children's wards in hospitals, raising the spirits of kids who had little laughter in their lives. She loved the work, but it paid little, and there were always so many other things to do, and so few hours in every day.

At last the detailed thoughts grew faint, pushed away by the hazy comfort of sleep. And when the dreams came, they weren't about details at all, nor about finding time; they were filled with a man whose blue eyes were so deep and so incredibly powerful that she thought, if she didn't take care, she might possibly drown in them.

And Peggy Shilling was an excellent swimmer.

Chapter Four

Wednesday dawned bright and sunny. Lake breezes blew in and fought off the June heat that was threatening to envelop the city. Peggy sponged up the mess of cereal Billy had fed to his toy bear, cleaned his chubby face and slipped a T-shirt over his head. "Carmen's coming today, Billy. Mommy's going to work. I have a wonderful new job."

"Ca-men," Billy said.

"Yes," Peggy answered as she began to look for a dress that would be appropriate for her first day at work with Kendrick Enterprises. She shoved aside her brilliantly colored clown outfits—bright purple and orange and pink silky blouses and baggy pants that she had found at estate sales—and sought out a semiconservative outfit a consultant would wear. The word made her smile. *Consultant.* Good grief, consultants were erudite men with wrinkles in their foreheads and smooth, rich-smelling attaché cases. They weren't Peggy Shillings. She wondered briefly if Kendrick Enterprises knew what they were doing when they hired her. And then she shrugged and laughed out loud. It wasn't her problem. She most certainly knew a heck of a lot more about people with problems than Mike Kendrick or Joe Paling. And that was the main issue here, after all. "Of course," she said, looking into the long, walnut-framed mirror that had belonged to her grandmother, "of course, of course, of course. I'm just the ticket, McQuicket, right, Billy boy?"

She winked at Billy through the mirror and he grinned so broadly his eyes turned into tiny slits.

"Such an audience you are, Billy. Don't ever leave me, promise?"

"Mama," he said and clapped his hands.

Peggy smiled and plucked a bright blue blouse from the closet. In minutes she was ready, her blouse tucked into the narrow waistband of a slim paisley skirt Casey had thrown her way. She had brushed her hair to a healthy shine and it hung full and loose just above her shoulders. She wet her lips, and then wondered briefly when she'd be able to replace the cosmetics Billy had donated to the city sewage system. Not for a while, she guessed; cosmetics were way down at the bottom on her must-buy-soon list.

Carmen breezed in a few minutes later and Peggy pushed some bills into her hand, explaining that she hadn't had time to stop at the market. Would Carmen mind picking up some milk and cereal and whatever she thought sounded good for lunch?

Carmen took the money and shoved it into her jeans. "We'll be fine, Peggy. Just go, get out and don't be late. This job sounds so terrific."

Peggy stopped at the door and looked over her shoulder at the baby-sitter. "You don't fool me for one second, Carmen. It's Mike Kendrick that has you getting here five minutes early and offering to stay late. I know your game."

"Well, God knows, Peggy, someone has to encourage you. You're a beautiful woman and you bury yourself here. This guy is a number-one catch!"

"Carmen, you're nuts! Mike Kendrick might as well live on Mars, that's how far apart we are. Find me someone within reach and we'll talk." She blew Billy a kiss, grabbed her purse and rushed out the door.

It wasn't until after the forty-minute bus drive to Michigan Avenue that Peggy realized she didn't know where to go. She stood in front of the now-familiar building with the mirrored facade and frowned. And then, checking her watch, she made a quick decision and headed inside and to the bank of elevators. She'd go to Michael's office, that was the sensible thing. And he'd direct her from there.

The secretary's desk was empty when Peg reached the elegant suite of offices. She glanced around. It was as quiet as a tomb. Beyond the ferns and ornate tables and chairs she noticed that Mike's office door was slightly ajar and a second later she heard the low cadence of his voice. She smiled. Good. At least they hadn't deserted her. She headed toward the door.

"Good morning," she said, pushing the door all the way open. Mike was seated at his desk, his hands folded behind his head. He was talking to a broad-shouldered, gray-haired man who had his back to her.

Peggy took a step backward. "Oh, I'm sorry, I didn't mean to interrupt."

Mike's face broke out into a welcoming smile. "No problem. Come on in, Peggy. I want you to meet—"

At that moment the gray-haired man turned around and looked at Peggy. His thick white brows pulled together.

Peggy's smile faded, then disappeared completely.

The man looked at her carefully with a vague expression of recognition. Then the scrutiny, the frown, turned into a deep grimace. "You! It's you! What the hell—"

Mike stood. He frowned and looked from Peggy to his father. "What's the problem, Dad?"

"Dad?" Peggy croaked.

"It's that fool girl I told you about who almost set me on fire!" the older man said.

Mike looked at Peggy, then back to his dad. Mike's face was calm, his voice even. "This is Peggy Shilling, Dad. We've hired her to help out on the documentary Joe is doing for—"

"Damn fool choice!" the elder Kendrick bellowed.

"Now wait a minute here, Mr. Kendrick," Peggy said, her face flushed but her voice strong. She held one hand up in the air as if to ward off blows. "That was an accident yesterday. I should have been more careful, I admit, but it has absolutely nothing to do with this job. It was an innocent mistake."

"Mistakes are never innocent," R.J. Kendrick IV intoned.

Peggy looked at him long and hard. She thought she saw a challenge in his eyes, but his words were so irritating. They were pompous and exaggerated and made her furious. She stood straighter, took a deep breath to calm herself and focused her mind on the new shoes she wanted to buy Billy. "Perhaps we should start over, Mr. Kendrick," she said pleasantly. "Let's pretend I didn't put out your cigar with my purse and that you didn't curse at me." She took a step forward and smiled sweetly, and then she held out her hand. "Hello, Mr. Kendrick, I'm Peggy Shilling. It's a pleasure to meet you."

R. J. Kendrick eyed her intently. His face was a hard, inscrutable mask. Peggy felt a crumbling inside, as if parts of her body were flaking off. His eyes were flat and gray and probing, his face still handsome beneath the lines and looseness of age. Finally he held out his hand and briefly, with a force that left her fingers tingling, he shook her hand. "Hello, Miss Shilling," he said gruffly, and without another word he stalked out of the office.

Peggy watched him walk away. Then slowly she turned toward Mike.

He was watching her with a mix of admiration and amusement. Few people stood up to his father. It wasn't just his power but the frightening strength of his gaze. The look that melted icebergs, his childhood friends used to say. But it didn't melt Peggy Shilling, at least not that he could see. He smiled. "Hi, Peggy," he said.

"Your father," she said slowly, the words stringing out across the room all the way to the door. She looked back to the door as if she half expected him to come back.

"Yes," Mike said. "That's my father."

"He was crazy about me," she said.

"I could tell. Is he the reason for that hole in your purse?"

"The cigar."

"We'll get you another one."

"No!" The word shot out into the air like a bullet. She sighed and spoke softly. "I mean, no, thank you. You don't owe me a purse."

"Well, it sounds as if my father does."

"No, neither does he. *I* bumped into him, Mike. I mean, this is crazy. I drop lasagna on your foot and you buy me dinner. I bump into your father and you want to buy me a purse. If tonight when I go home I accidentally burn down my apartment house, will you buy me another?"

Mike sat in the tall-backed leather chair and looked at her with a level gaze that stopped her words. "I'm sorry my father upset you," he said simply.

Peggy was still. He had ignored her words and zeroed in on her feelings. It made her uncomfortable. "I'm sorry I went on like that, but I guess he did upset me. He doesn't know me well enough to speak to me that way."

"No, he doesn't. But he isn't awful, Peggy. He simply demands from people what he expects from himself."

"Perfection."

Mike laughed softly. "Precisely," he said. "Now, would you like a cup of coffee?"

"No, no, thank you. I came here because I wasn't sure where I was to meet Mr. Paling. He mentioned a meeting...."

"First off, it's Joe. You call him Mr. Paling and he'll be depressed for a week. As for the meeting, it's in an hour over in a warehouse Joe uses for props. I told him I'd get you over there."

Peggy frowned, then shook her head. "Listen, Mike, I can find it myself if you give me directions. I...I appreciate the job—I really do. And Billy, he appreciates it, too." She smiled, then grew serious again. "You probably went out on a limb for me. I'm grateful for that, even if I'm not sure why. But I don't want to put you out anymore. I can carry the ball from here—"

The intercom interrupted her ill-thought-out speech and she was relieved. Mike had been sitting calmly in his chair, listening carefully, but he seemed more entertained by what she was saying than anything else. When he hung up and turned his attention back to her, she smiled brightly. "So, sir—the directions, please?" She tilted her head back in what she hoped was a casual but businesslike way and hoped he would stop looking at her so intently. It caused odd sensations—first cold, then hot rushes—to travel along her spine.

"It makes you uncomfortable to have me help you, doesn't it?"

The question caught her off guard because he had done it again—cut right through the facade and gone to her feelings. She looked out the window and watched the brilliant streaks of white sunshine crest along the lake, riding the waves like ephemeral surfers. Finally she looked back at Mike. He was quiet, his blue-black eyes still holding her. She thought for a minute that she couldn't leave now even if she wanted to. His eyes had bound her, frozen her right there on the muted Oriental rug. "I cherish my independence," she said quietly.

Mike nodded. "I know you do. That's just one of the things that intrigues me about you."

"But I'm not ungrateful."

"I know that, too." He forked a hand through his thick dark hair and finally smiled, a slight, crooked smile that caused Peggy to expel a lungful of caught air. *Damn, he is handsome when he does that.* She almost wished his father would walk back in. At least the elderly Mr. Kendrick created an atmosphere she could deal with.

Mike shoved back his chair and stood. "I'll tell you what I'll do, Peg. I'll let you buy me breakfast. How's that for respecting your independence?"

"Well—"

"And then I'll drop you off at the warehouse as I had intended to do, since I have a meeting nearby."

Mike was around his desk and picking up an attaché case from the conference table before Peggy could reply. He held open the office door and gestured for her to go through. "Shall we?"

There wasn't anything to say, any answer that didn't sound foolish, so Peggy walked through the door, vowing that she'd put some perspective on all this as soon as she had a little time. Most of her thoughts, however, were focused on a more immediate concern:

How in heaven's name were the seven bus tokens in her purse going to pay for Mike's breakfast?

JOE PALING and Michael Kendrick, friends for over half their lives, sat in the dimly lit bar at the Drake Hotel and ordered drinks. As soon as the waitress disappeared, Joe answered Mike's unspoken question.

"She's as smart as a whip, irreverent as hell and adds a hell of a lot of spice to this project."

"Good. You can use her, then."

"Sure. She has some good ideas, some fresh approaches to things." Joe watched Mike light up his pipe. "But just for the record, buddy, what do you owe her? What sort of sin are you making amends for?"

Mike frowned and then a brief flash of anger crossed his face.

"Sorry," Joe said quickly. "I guess that's out of line. It's your business. Besides, I like her. She's not only smart but has a great sense of humor, so I should be thanking you instead of examining your motives."

"That's right." Mike sat back in the chair and looked at Joe. He and Joe had been friends for way too long to misread each other. "If you want the honest-to-God truth, Joe," he said slowly, "I don't know why I hired her. It seemed to happen on its own. There's something about her—I mean, I find myself saying things to her that I hadn't thought out ahead of time."

"Not at all like you, Mike."

"That's right." Mike shifted his shoulders beneath the suit jacket, easing the tense muscles. "I don't know, hell, maybe it was my good deed for the day. She has this baby to support...."

"Again, not exactly like you, Mike."

Mike laughed. "Actually, there's nothing more to it. She's an attractive young woman, and she intrigued me when I met her. But that's all. And I'm glad she's contributing to the project."

Joe said quietly, watching his friend. "And that's really all?"

Mike was silent for a moment, his eyes following the wavy lines in the polished wood table. Then he looked up at his friend and laughed. "Yeah, that's all. Although, damn, she does get to me, somehow. I don't know what it is. Maybe it's the novelty of someone so different, so unimpressed with the usual things. And so honest. She was going on about being independent yesterday so I told her she could take me to breakfast, never thinking that she might not be able to afford it." He laughed at the memory, shook his head and then went on. "She excused herself after we ate and I saw her talking to the hostess in the hallway. I didn't think much about it until we were leaving and Peggy slipped into the ladies' room for a minute. The hostess came looking for her and since she wasn't there, she left the message with me. It was a receipt from the manager for Peggy's watch. She had left it with him as collateral, promising to bring the money in for the meal as soon as she could."

Joe laughed. "I like her. And I think you've met your match in Peggy Shilling."

"Mismatch is more like it. But I do like her. She has definite flair."

"That she does," agreed Joe.

As Joe flagged down a waiter, Mike drifted into further thoughts about Peggy. Thinking about her brought unexpected pleasure to him, just as talking to her had done during breakfast the day before. Being with Peggy made him feel as if he were on vacation. It was nice. Very nice.

"Over here, ladies," Joe was saying across from him, his voice traveling above the murmurs of conversation in the lounge. Mike looked up, feeling oddly disoriented for a minute. Joe was half-standing, motioning toward two elegant-looking women who had just walked in. "Nancy, over here," Joe repeated.

Mike frowned. "Who...?"

Joe glanced at him, a look of amusement on his face. "Our dates, Mike. Remember?"

"Yes, sure," he said, then grinned crookedly a second before the two women joined them at the small table. Mike stood and kissed Melanie Hudson on the cheek and forced his mind back to the moment, to the dark, crowded lounge and the two very beautiful women gracing their table.

"Michael, you're looking very dazed tonight. Long day?" Melanie rested her long, tapered fingers on his hand.

"Dazzled by your beauty, Mel, that's all."

Melanie laughed and ordered her drink. She and Michael had known each other practically since birth, and explanations weren't necessary for moods. They had dated on and off for a long time, and were regular companions for one another on their crowded social calendars even though they both dated others, as well. The Hudsons and the Kendricks were considered equals in the social stratum in which they lived, and both families had made it clear they wouldn't mind marriage ties. Michael, however, felt sure Melanie loved him the same way he loved her—as an old friend, not as a marriage partner. "Nancy and I had a little trouble getting here," Melanie said now. "There's a protest going on on Michigan Avenue and it fouled up traffic."

"Protest?" Joe said.

"Yes," Nancy Spaulding answered. Nancy, at the age of thirty, was one of Cook County's wealthiest, most beautiful and most successful hostesses. She was also very short-tempered when it came to others' frailties. Her eyebrows drew together now at the thought of the protesters, and her large, perfectly lined eyes darkened. "It's ridiculous. There's a developers' seminar at the Park Hyatt and one of the issues is the tearing down of those dilapidated buildings on Whitney Street in order to put in a state-of-the-art mall. Apparently there's a group against it and they're lined up outside handing out materials explaining their cause."

"Sounds innocent enough," Joe said. "A lot of people will lose their homes if that plan goes through."

"Maybe," Nancy went on. "But it *looks* awful. So vulgar. There are stacks of cardboard boxes with flyers all over and it's difficult for people shopping or going to dinner to get by."

"Land of the free," Michael said. "It's why we live here and not China."

"True," Melanie said. "But Nancy means there might be other ways to do it. Something not so..."

"So visible," Nancy said, satisfied with her neat solution. "They should organize a committee."

"I'm sure they do have committees, Nancy," Michael offered.

"No, I mean *real* committees. You should have seen them, Michael. They have ragged jeans on, for heaven's sake, and some even have children with them. Who would possibly listen to them, take them even halfway seriously, looking like that?"

"Perhaps," Melanie said, "if they appeared more professional, more organized and made an appointment at the mayor's office or with the developers, they'd be more effective."

"Usually those groups want to hit the voters, educate the masses, as much as anything else," Mike said. "And chances are they wouldn't get anywhere near the developer no matter how many meetings they asked for."

"Oh, it's not difficult at all to set up meetings with people," Nancy said with a dismissing wave of her hand. "But whatever, they'll probably all end up in jail, anyway. Now let's talk about more important things, like the committee Melanie and I are on for the circus-ball benefit for Children's Hospital. We've generously signed up the two of you to help out with it."

Mike frowned and began to shake his head but Melanie spoke quickly. "She's half joking, Michael.

I know you don't have a lot of time for this sort of thing but the Junior League is sponsoring it and it's also your mother's favorite charity.''

Mike's frown deepened.

Joe laughed. ''Well, that settles that. Not only will Michael be in attendance but every Kendrick within seven states able to breathe on his own will be there as well. Claire Kendrick does have a way of twisting one's arm.''

''That's why she's such a wonderful volunteer. Charities couldn't survive without people like Mrs. Kendrick,'' said Nancy.

Melanie looked sideways at Mike. ''Don't worry, love, we'll keep your involvement to a minimum. Nancy and I are heading a committee and mostly we'll need moral support and handsome escorts.''

''Now you're talking my language,'' Joe said affably, reordering drinks for everyone. ''That's our expertise. Besides, the food ought to be great.''

''The way to Joe's heart,'' Nancy said as the group laughed and conversation turned to mutual friends, to vacations and to a possible fall trip to Antibes.

Mike sat back and watched, listened with one ear, and wondered what Peggy and Billy were doing. Sitting in that tiny living room probably, playing and laughing, Peggy pretending Billy understood every word she said. Or perhaps they'd gone to the market; Peggy said she and Billy often did that at night—cheap entertainment, she called it. Billy absolutely loved the grocery carts, the colors and commotion, and especially the man behind the fish counter who always juggled a couple of catfish for Billy's entertainment.

They would eat free samples from the trays held out by elderly women, who made a wonderful fuss over Billy, and then they'd both come home exhausted and full. Or maybe they had stayed home and were seated in the one big chair in the apartment, curled up reading a book together, Billy's curly blond head pressed against Peggy's bosom. Well, wherever they were, one thing was certain—they were definitely not planning a million-dollar fund-raising extravaganza or a trip to Antibes.

"Michael?"

He looked up with a start. The others were standing, looking down at him. Melanie was watching him with a peculiar expression on her face.

"What?" Mike forked his fingers through his hair and then stood. He laughed lightly. "Sorry. Are we leaving?"

"We have reservations for dinner, darling," Melanie said. "I need to get home early tonight. Are you all right?"

"Michael has had a lot on his mind lately. New commitment, that sort of thing. Let's not give him a hard time," Joe said. He began to hustle the women through the crowded lounge, then looked back at Michael with a crooked grin on his face.

"Thanks, Joe," Mike said in a low voice, and then in one long swallow he drained his drink, put the glass back on the table and wove his way through the crowded bar and out into the clear Chicago night.

IT WAS LATER THAT NIGHT, after he had taken Melanie home, that Mike finally relaxed. He dropped his jacket onto a chair, pulled off his tie and fixed himself a drink, then switched on the television in the glass-walled den of his comfortable lakeshore home and settled himself in an oversize chair. Beyond the windows the lake lapped soothingly against the shore and the black sky calmed him. The late news came on and he half listened to it as his mind drifted back over the evening. It had been pleasant enough—a good dinner, congenial conversation, some laughs. They had had dozens of similar evenings together, the four of them, but for reasons that escaped him Mike had found his mind wandering frequently this night and it was only through Joe's efforts that he didn't come across as rude or uninterested. He didn't know what was causing the restlessness, the fogginess, the inability to concentrate, but he was relieved when Melanie suggested they call it a night.

He lifted his feet onto the ottoman now, leaned his head back into the chair cushions and listened to the newscaster's carefully modulated voice work its way through the day's events in the life of the teeming city. He watched, detached, as criminals were arrested before his eyes, as weather was reported and as the Chicago Cubs won a game.

And then, as the cameras switched to a recorded Mini cam report of a local meeting, Mike jerked upright in his chair.

There she was, filling the screen of his television, as real as if she were here in this room seated a few feet from him.

Peggy.

She was calm, smiling, her arms holding an enormous pile of flyers, and Billy was there, too. His sturdy body was strapped to Peggy's narrow back and his blond head bobbed happily to the rhythm of the clattering, noisy crowd. He was grinning and his small fingers played lightly with his mother's hair.

Peggy was talking to the reporter, her eyes spilling bright light and her voice friendly and articulate. It was a meeting, she explained carefully, to decide the fate of over a hundred residents, mostly elderly, who lived in the historic area and who hadn't much say as to their destiny. Builders wanted to replace their small, unassuming homes with a Saks and a Bonwit's and an expensive French restaurant. She and the others who were peacefully handing out information sheets simply wanted people to know, wanted them to have the information they needed to form an opinion on the action before it was too late.

Mike watched her, transfixed. She had on blue jeans and a bright pink T-shirt that had a simple horizon drawing of the quaint old houses in the neighborhood and above it the words Home Sweet Home.

He thought of Nancy and Melanie and their disapproval of the inelegant protesters. *Some even have children with them,* Nancy had said. And then he shook his head and a smile eased the lines of his face. On television, Peggy was telling the reporter, who was obviously smitten with her, what the group she represented would like interested people to do.

Well, he'd been wrong about one thing, Mike thought. Peggy hadn't spent the night curled up in a chair reading to Billy. And as the images on the screen shifted and the weatherman came back for a final forecast, another thought occurred to him. There were an awful lot of things about Peggy that he didn't know, many things he'd guess wrong on. It was a curious observation, followed up by a very pleasurable decision—he'd simply have to devote a little more time to finding out some of those unknowns.

Chapter Five

If he hadn't had a company to buy at two and a news-paper to sell an hour later, Mike would have been content to sit on the hard, uncomfortable park bench for the rest of the day and do nothing but watch the light dance in Peggy Shilling's amazing green eyes. Reluctantly he stood and stretched his arms over his head.

"Don't forget your jacket," Peggy said, picking up the smooth summer-weight coat from the back of the bench. She stood beside him, squinting up into the bright sunlight.

Peggy and Mike had somehow happened to have had lunch together nearly every day for two weeks. It was always on one pretense or another—Mike check-ing with Joe about this or that, a lawyer's meeting nearby that brought him to the area or Peggy suggest-ing she pack a picnic lunch. Sometimes Joe came along but most often it was just the two of them, sit-ting at a counter in a diner on State Street or, when Mike could talk her into it, a more leisurely luncheon in the cool, leather booths of a fine restaurant.

Mike didn't know why he did it. It was counterproductive. He had enormous responsibilities running a multimillion-dollar corporation, and lunching with employees of Kendrick Enterprises wasn't something he usually did. But here he was—again—sitting in the shade of a giant sycamore tree in a small park near the lake, wondering what it was about Peggy that eased the day and helped wash away the summer heat.

"Your jacket, sir?" Peggy said again.

"Thanks, Peggy." He took the jacket, then looked over at the lake as if there were some taskmaster there, someone giving him instructions. "I need to run," he said finally as he looked back at Peggy.

"Oh, sure, I know you do, Mike." She smiled.

"I have a string of meetings a mile long this afternoon." He swung his jacket over one shoulder.

"And I have a bus to catch. Joe doesn't need me anymore today, so I'm going to bask in the luxury of a few free hours and take Billy swimming at a park near my apartment."

Mike listened, and then he thought about her apartment, about the traffic and smells that filled the small spaces between the buildings. He thought about the groups of kids hanging around the congested street corners and he wondered what such a neighborhood park would be like.

He looked at her. "I have a better idea, Peggy."

Peggy's brows went up into her bangs. "Let me guess. Billy and I could attend your meetings with you." She shook her head, feigning disappointment. "Sorry, Mike. Billy would love it but I have a thing about meetings."

"Well, too bad. Can you bear to pass up the current trends in fiscal management?"

"Only with great reluctance." She laughed into the white sunshine.

"Let me throw out another idea, then, one you can't pass up."

"Go for it." Peggy stood just in front of him, listening intently.

"Okay, try this one on. My place isn't too far from here and it not only has a pool but a beach, as well. You'd have your choice and Billy would love it."

Peggy frowned.

"There's no one there, Peg. All that water and no one uses it."

"Why not?"

"I don't have time. You and Billy can go in, make yourself at home. Billy can swim nude if he wants. And you don't have to worry about...well, about the pool being too crowded. Sometimes those public neighborhood pools get hectic on hot summer days."

"Now how would you know that, Mike Kendrick?" Peggy had her hands on her hips now, her head tilted back, and her eyes were laughing as she looked up at him. "I bet you've never been in a public pool in your whole life."

Mike thought for a minute. Then he lifted one brow. "Does the one in college count?"

"You call a Harvard pool *public?* Wrong, Kendrick."

"Oh." Mike shoved his hands in his pockets and leaned his head to one side, watching her. "Well, okay, you win. I've never been in a public pool. But I read the papers. My own newspapers publish pictures of crowded pools in the summer. I know these things." He held her still with his eyes. "So, what do you think, Peggy? It's silly not to use it. Say but the word and it's yours."

Peggy paused for a minute. It was a terrific invitation. Billy would love it, and if she took Carmen along they'd each get a chance to sit and do nothing for a while. "Does the bus go that way?" she asked.

He nodded.

Peggy chewed thoughtfully on her bottom lip. She wanted to teach Billy how to swim this summer. It would be great to start the process in a quiet place. Besides, the neighborhood pool often had green things growing on its walls.

Mike looked toward his car, then back to Peggy. "Well, I've got to go, Peg. If you change your mind, call my office."

"No, wait." Peggy rested one arm on his sleeve. "It's a wonderful, generous offer. I guess . . . I guess I just don't know how much of your niceness I should start depending on, you know?"

Mike looked puzzled and Peggy went on. "I mean, I don't want to become spoiled—"

"I don't think a couple of hours in a private pool would spoil you, Peggy."

"Well, no, maybe not. And that's why I'm going to say yes. I accept your kindness. Billy and I would love to be royalty for an afternoon. Why not!"

CARMEN WAS AS THRILLED as Billy. She threw a couple of her college textbooks into a brightly colored bag and followed Peggy down the stairs.

"I checked the schedule and we can take the train on up," Peggy said. "It shouldn't be more than a twenty-minute ride."

"It sounds great, Peggy," Carmen said. And then she tickled Billy's chin and their laughter bounced off the thin walls of the stairwell.

"What's his house like?" Carmen asked as they settled themselves on the hard plastic seats of the northbound train.

"I don't have the faintest idea," Peggy said. "It's probably ultrachic, filled with glass and chrome. Stark, you know, and decorated very precisely by some high-priced Michigan Avenue firm."

"The perfect bachelor pad," Carmen said.

"Yes," Peggy said. She looked out the window as she let her mind elaborate on this house that would be the place Mike Kendrick called home.

THEY HAD TROUBLE AT FIRST finding the house. The street was easy to find, but the houses were all tucked back behind thickets of bushes and trees and surrounded by wrought-iron fences. Finally Carmen spotted 402, the numbers displayed discreetly on a small brass plate and fastened to a short post beside the brick walkway. The front of the property was bordered by bushes and trees, so thick that it looked more like a forest than a yard. Carmen and Peggy walked through the gates and down the short walkway several yards before the trees thinned out to reveal the house.

Peggy's breath caught in her throat. "Oh, my," she finally breathed. It was an English manor house, enchanting and lovely, complete with flower boxes, chimneys and lead leaders on the many casement windows.

"Some bachelor pad," Carmen murmured as the threesome made their way tentatively toward the front door.

"Maybe it's the family home," Peggy whispered. "It must be. One person couldn't live here. Do you think we should go back?"

"Absolutely not," Carmen said.

Peggy laughed and took a step up to the door. She rang the bell first, and when no one answered she inserted the key that Mike had given her into the brass lock and said a quick prayer that Mr. R. J. Kendrick or Michael's mother wouldn't be standing there. But when the door swung open there was only an empty foyer in front of them, a beautiful entry that drew them into its shadowed splendor.

The interior of the house was cool and lovely and fresh smelling and Peggy walked on toward the back of the house, drawn by the light that spilled from windows visible from the hallway. Carmen, with Billy in her arms, followed.

They found themselves in a den, a large, comfortable room filled with walls of books, oversize, worn chairs and a fireplace. It smelled of leather and pipes and after-shave. *Mike,* Peggy thought and she smiled. Yes, this room was Mike. And instinctively she knew his parents didn't live here with him; he lived here all alone.

"Oh, Peggy, look," Carmen was saying and Peggy looked ahead, opposite them, where a wall full of windows framed a stone-lined, meandering swimming pool, and beyond it, down a winding pathway lined with evergreen trees, the lake.

"Wawa," Billy squealed.

"Heaven," Peggy whispered.

"Fantastic," Carmen said.

It took an hour to explore, down the wooden steps to the private beach, then up again to the pool and the pool house where Peggy found rubber rafts and life jackets and a cabinet full of sun lotions. It also had a stocked bar, an elegant dressing room, a pile of white fluffy towels and a closet with beach robes and extra suits.

"Peggy, I'm never leaving," said Carmen, settling herself into a chaise longue.

Peggy sat on the fan of steps that led down into the pool and buckled a life belt around Billy. "I think that'd be fine, Carmen. I'll just explain to Mike that you're this mermaid who happened to be washed up on shore. I'm sure he'll take good care of you." She supported Billy between her legs and began to rub sun protection lotion on his cheeks and shoulders.

"Mike's taking good care of *you*, Peggy, that's for sure," Carmen said and then she closed her eyes and stretched her slender dark legs out in front of her.

The words settled inside Peggy's head and she thought about them while she lowered Billy into the water. Carmen was wrong, of course. Mike wasn't

taking care of her, he was simply extending hospital-
ity. She wasn't sure why he was even doing *that,* but he
wasn't taking care of her. No one had ever taken care
of Peggy, not really. Her father had always been busy
at the factory, and her mother had treated Peggy more
like a friend than a daughter. At times Peggy had re-
sented that, but she knew that somehow that was what
her mother needed to keep her going, a moral support, not a dependent. So Peggy had fulfilled the role
as best she could. She liked being independent, especially when she saw the results of not being so. Her
mother was so dependent on her father that when he
died, she fell apart. During those difficult years after
his death Peggy had vowed never to let herself be that
reliant on another person. And she had faithfully and
proudly lived up to that vow.

"Mama," Billy said, pulling her thoughts back to
the splashes and kicks coming from her son. He
plunged his head into the water, then jerked it back up,
water spurting from his grinning mouth.

Peggy grinned. "You're terrific, Billy! From now on
I will call you Fish," she said. She held his round rump
in the palm of one hand as he trustingly lay back upon
the water, his smooth, pink shoulders dipping gently
beneath the water, and then they both giggled as she
moved him like a small sailboat across the pool.

"My turn," Carmen said a while later. She slid her
lean body cautiously into the pool, then took Billy
from his mother and glided with him across the water. "Why do you suppose he has this place?" she
asked Peggy.

"Who?"

"Mike, of course."

"This house? Well, why not?"

"It's so enormous, Peggy. Was he married?"

Peggy shrugged. She didn't know. She didn't know if he was married, if he had kids; only instinct told her he lived there alone. And the fact that she *didn't* know these things startled her briefly. It belied the closeness she felt when she was with Mike.

She felt she knew him, that they were good friends, and yet they had rarely talked about these important things. She wondered now, as she floated out into the middle of the pool, if that was on purpose. Maybe Mike had purposely steered the conversation away from things that would be personal, so that their relationship would remain more professional, more realistic. She hooked her elbows behind her, up on the tiled side of the pool, and let her feet swim out in front of her body. Yes, that was probably it.

"Use this, Peggy," Carmen said, and she sent a long raft floating Peggy's way. Peggy eased herself up on it, stretched out on her back and laughed as Carmen with Billy in tow pushed her across the pool. And then she drifted off by herself, the raft moving along the currents that came from Carmen and Billy's splashing. Her eyes were closed and the white sun beat down on her, easing the tensions and worries of life out of her body. She was limp, a sleepy rag doll, she thought. And it felt absolutely delicious.

"IT'S WONDERFUL," she murmured some time later.

"What is?" asked a deep, friendly voice beside her.

"Hmm, this. Relaxing…being here at Mike's.…" And then a cold chill swept through Peggy. "Carmen?" she whispered. Slowly she pulled her eyes open. She saw the sky first. The sun had moved from over her head to back behind the trees and the house. Long shadows lay across the green-blue water. At the side of the pool, several feet from her face, were long, bare, male feet. Her heart stopped. *Where is Billy!*

She sat up abruptly and the rubber raft immediately folded in two, sending her, with wildly flailing arms, into the water.

In an instant Mike was in the pool and at her side. He slipped his arms around her and pulled her to the steps at the shallow end of the pool.

"Mike," she sputtered. "Where is Billy? What happened? What are you doing here?"

With one arm still around her waist, Mike brushed the hair away from her eyes. "Billy and Carmen are building a sand castle down on the beach, you fell asleep, and I live here."

Peggy took a deep breath and slipped out of his arms. Gentle waves lapped against her breasts as she slid down onto a middle step. She pressed her hand to her chest, forcing her heartbeat into submission. "I guess you startled me," she said with a small smile. "I'm sorry."

"I should be sorry. I found you out here when I got home, this gorgeous sea creature floating across my pool, and you looked far too peaceful to disturb. So I wandered down to the beach and helped Carmen and Billy build the Taj Mahal. It's pretty good."

She smiled. "Billy has never been on a beach before."

"I gathered that. Carmen and I finally convinced him we have better things here to eat than sand."

"Are they still down there?"

"They were on their way up. Carmen was going to take Billy inside to change him and get him some apple juice."

"You have apple juice in this house?"

"We aim to please, ma'am," Mike said and then slipped down beside her on the steps and leaned back, his elbows on the step above, his laughing eyes warming her face. She tried to focus on his smile, to keep her gaze clear of his body, but she found it nearly impossible. His chest, broad and covered with dark, springy hair that angled down to his flat abdomen, was just inches away from her. He did nothing to evade her gaze. Instead he just sat there, leaning back, perfectly at ease, supremely confident . . . incredibly sexy.

A chill ran through her.

"What's the matter?" Mike asked.

"Nothing," she said quickly. Peggy looked ahead and stared at the raft. It was floating riderless now across the pool. "I haven't seen you this way before, I mean without clothes on."

Mike grinned. "I guess not."

"I mean without a suit on. You have clothes on, of course."

"Of course." He moved one long leg beneath the water. "It's easier to swim this way, without a suit and tie, I mean."

Peggy sighed. "This is an inane conversation."

"Unsuitable, you mean."

Peggy groaned. "I hate puns, Mike."

"Okay, sorry. I thought it would relax you. You seem tense. I don't think of you as tense."

"I am tense, it is unusual, and I don't like it."

"Well, relax," he said, shifting so he could see her better. "Here, this always works. Turn a little." He placed one hand on each of her shoulders and began to move his fingers in slow, sure strokes. His thumbs grazed her shoulder blades, then pressed easily into her skin, kneading it slowly.

At first Peggy tensed up, but in minutes her head fell back and she closed her eyes. "Mike, that feels absolutely wonderful," she said. "You could charge for it."

"I do," he said, and Peggy colored slightly, pretending she hadn't heard. Her skin was slippery and his hands felt wonderful as they glided across her upper back, down between her shoulder blades, then up over her shoulders and along the column of her neck. She felt fluid, like the water in the pool.

When a small sigh slipped from beneath her lips, Mike said, "There. That's called Kendrick's magic massage, guaranteed to cure what ails you."

Peggy smiled. "It did. Thanks." She stretched out, leaning against the steps until the water came up to her neck. "We've had a great time here today."

"Good, then you won't think it was presumptuous of me to tell Stella you'd stay for dinner."

"Stella? Is that your mother?"

Mike laughed heartily now, from deep in his throat. Then he explained, "No, Stella is my cook. She lives over the garage. My mother's name is Claire, and I don't think she has ever cooked anything in her life. Once my father bought her a copper colander because a clerk in the store talked him into it, and my mother planted a geranium in it."

Peggy's laughter rippled across the water.

"So you'll stay?" he said, but it wasn't really a question, Peggy realized. It was more a confirmation of something already decided.

"All three of us?"

"Carmen and Billy are staying—they already RSVP'd. You're the only unknown."

"I guess I will, then. I can't go home without them."

"Good."

"And your cook . . . doesn't mind?"

"Stella is happy as a clam. She hasn't seen her grandchildren in nearly a year—they live in California—so Billy is receiving all her pent-up grandmotherly affection. And Carmen was telling her the best way to make enchiladas—something about corn husks."

"So everyone is happy," Peggy mused. She lifted herself up on the step.

"One can only hope." He smiled then, a crooked, sexy, confident smile that teased Peggy into action. With one swift movement of limbs that were strong from carrying groceries and a twenty-five-pound toddler, she pushed down on Mike Kendrick's broad, wonderful shoulders until he was completely submerged in the water of his pool.

He went down, but not without a fight, and before Peggy knew it her ankle was fastened in an iron grip and her body was sliding off the steps and into the center of the pool. When she finally opened her eyes beneath the water, there he was, his dark hair slightly longer than an executive's should be, his eyes laughing. They surfaced together, their arms treading the water in support, and Peggy shook her head in the afternoon air, her laughter skimming across the water. "You're crazy, Kendrick."

"You started this, don't forget." His long fingers curled around her waist, and before she could get away Mike lifted her into the air and sent her flying back into the water.

"War!" she shouted as she emerged above water once again. And she flung her reedlike body through the water toward him.

But Mike was too quick for her this time and he caught her, holding her tight against his chest. His added height allowed him to stand on the bottom, but Peggy was at his mercy. His arms encircled her waist, and her breasts, covered only by the thin wet suit, were flattened against his chest. For a second Peggy was stunned, and then her head reeled at the onslaught of emotion. She wanted more than anything to tilt her head back, to look into the depths of those incredible midnight blue eyes and to kiss him. "Mike," she tried to say, but the single word came out in a sigh.

Mike smiled. He kept one arm around her waist, and his other hand went up to her hair, his fingers sliding over the silky strands. And then he kissed her, his lips covering hers, his tongue slipping easily inside her mouth.

Peggy felt hot and cold at once, an incredible blend of sensations that swept through her and swirled around like a whirlpool, all the way down into the very center of her.

"Hey, where are you two?" a voice shouted in the distance. "It's time to dry off for dinner."

Mike didn't let her go. Instead he moved wordlessly to the edge of the pool and lifted her easily up onto the side.

Peggy simply looked at him, her eyes wide, her mouth still slightly open.

"Hungry?" Mike asked. Then he braced his hands on the side of the pool and with athletic agility he swung himself up beside her and stood.

Peggy took the hand he offered and allowed him to pull her to her feet. But before she could say anything, Carmen appeared at the edge of the patio carrying a silver tray.

"You have two minutes to get dressed," she said to both of them, "or I'm going to eat every one of these myself." She looked with longing at the assortment of stuffed grape leaves and flaky Greek pastries that filled the tray.

"Where's Billy?" Peggy managed to say, her heart still pounding.

"He's in the kitchen with Stella. Now hurry," she said. A deep frown shadowed her face. "I mean it, I'll eat every one."

Mike laughed, then plucked two cheese pastries off the tray and gave one to Peggy before she hurried off to the pool house to change.

A quick, cool shower helped somewhat to restore Peggy's equilibrium, and when she walked back to the patio a short time later she had almost convinced herself the whole thing had been a dream, a wild imaginative fling she'd indulged in while floating across the pool on the rubber raft.

But when she spotted Mike, his hair still wet, his body dressed now in a knit sports shirt and khaki slacks, she was less sure. And when he looked up and smiled at her, that slow, crooked smile, she knew the kiss had definitely been real. There were some things even her active imagination couldn't fabricate.

Dinner was served on the terrace, a beautiful, flower-lined flagstone area off the living room. Stella, Mike's incredible cook and housekeeper, had not only come up with a high chair for Billy but had also come up with a meal that Peggy couldn't stop exclaiming over. She pulled a piece of the delicately herbed chicken from a bone and set it on Billy's tray. "Mike, you are the luckiest person alive," she said, and she smiled up at Stella, who was fussing over Billy.

"Stella is one in a million," he agreed.

"Oh, go on with you," Stella said, putting a small dish of lemon noodles in front of Billy. Then she disappeared inside to begin putting together the dessert.

"Carmen, Peggy tells me you're in college," Mike said.

Carmen laughed. "It's my sixth year. Peggy tells me I'm making a career out of it but she's wrong. One of these days I'll finish," she replied.

"I kid her, but she'll graduate, and with honors," Peggy said. She took a piece of warm garlic toast from the basket. "And when she does, Carmen will be the best schoolteacher in the Midwest."

"Yep," Carmen said, and then laughed at her own immodesty. "But I can't imagine not caring for Billy. He's the best. Do you have any kids, Mike?"

Peggy threw her a silencing look but Carmen artfully avoided her employer's grimace.

"Nope, no kids, Carmen. No wife, either."

"Not ever?" Carmen lifted her brows. Peggy kicked her beneath the table.

"Not ever so far."

"But you're not a confirmed bachelor?" Peggy kicked harder and Carmen winced.

"You okay?" Mike asked Carmen.

"Fine," Carmen answered, reaching down with one hand to rub her shin. "It must have been a hunger pain. So, where were we now—oh, the confirmed bachelor..."

Peggy sighed and handed Billy a roll.

"I never say never to anything, Carmen," Mike said, leaning back in the chair and clasping his hands behind his head, "so I guess you wouldn't say I was a confirmed bachelor. I like to leave things open, not close doors. It makes life more interesting."

"A man after my own heart. It's too bad you're not younger."

"And what difference does age make?" Mike asked philosophically.

Carmen leaned forward, her elbows pressed lightly into the edge of the table. "Well, let's explore this a little."

"This is a silly conversation," Peggy interjected, but neither Carmen nor Mike paid any attention to her.

"I'm twenty-three," Carmen said, "and you must be...what? Thirty?"

Mike grinned. Peggy noticed a dimple flash in his left cheek. He was relaxed and enjoying himself.

"Carmen, you're either not very observant or you think I want to be younger than I am."

"Okay, okay," Carmen said, her hands flapping through the air. "You're thirty-four, right?"

"On the button."

Carmen grinned. "Probably an Aquarian," she said.

"Amazing," Mike said.

"No, not so amazing. She probably asked Stella," Peggy said. She glowered at Carmen.

Carmen shrugged and then looked back at Mike. "Aquarians make good lovers."

"Carmen!"

Billy's banging on the wooden tray of the high chair was a welcome intrusion. Peggy scooped him up out of the chair and announced that she was going inside to change him.

But at that moment Stella appeared with a pink-and-white frothy concoction that stopped Peggy in her tracks.

"Strawberry crème à la Stella," the portly cook announced as she placed it on the table. "And Billy comes with me." Her smile allowed no argument and Billy was swept off into the house as Carmen began serving up the dessert.

Mike poured each of them a glass of wine, then settled back. "Sometimes I eat out here alone," Mike said, "but it's much nicer with this company." He smiled at each of the women in turn. Behind him, the sun was sinking down behind the trees.

Peggy sipped her wine. She looked around the terrace, cool now as the evening shadows fell across the flagstone. "It's absolutely gorgeous here, Mike, with or without people. It's...it's serene. So quiet and lovely. But..."

"What?"

"Well, it's none of my business, but why do you live here alone?"

Carmen pushed back her chair and stood. She grinned at Peggy. "Here you go, Peggy, asking all these personal questions. It embarrasses me. I think I'll go see if Stella needs help." And she disappeared, taking her dessert and wineglass with her.

Peggy shook her head. "She's so subtle."

"I get the feeling Carmen cares a lot for you and Billy."

"It's definitely mutual. Carmen is part of our family. I don't know what I'd have done without her this past year."

"Being a single parent must be difficult."

"Being a parent is difficult. But it's a wonderful kind of difficult. I wouldn't trade it for anything in the world. I only hope I can give Billy what he needs."

"You give him abundant love, that's obvious."

"Oh, sure, that I can do. And I agree, that's the most important thing. But I worry about taking care of his material needs, too. I mean, there are plenty of couples wanting to adopt who have a lot of money. I don't, and that's a problem sometimes." She smiled up at him then. "But you've helped me out there with this job, Mike. I'm grateful for that."

"Glad it worked out."

"We visited the home yesterday and Emily, the woman in charge, trusted Joe and the crew, I think."

"Because of you, from what Joe told me."

"Maybe, I don't know. Emily knows how I feel about the work she does with battered women, and she knows I wouldn't jeopardize it. But Joe was very sensitive in his approach."

"Good."

"Do you do any work with the filming?"

"No, I don't have time anymore. I used to fool around with it for fun, but now I do more in the main office."

"Running the show."

"In a way, although my father is still the ruling force there."

"He's a force, that much I'll vouch for."

Mike laughed. "He's a powerful man, but he can't handle the load he used to, so I'm taking on more."

Peggy leaned forward, her arms on the table and her expression intense. "Do you like it? The power, I mean, the big business, all that buying and selling."

"Like it?" Mike frowned. "I never thought about it like that before—like or dislike—but sure, I guess I do. I wasn't forced into it."

"You seem . . . well, you're more laid-back than my image of a mogul."

Mike's frown disappeared and he laughed. "Peggy, for being a liberated young woman, you're very hung up on stereotypes."

Peggy considered the thought. "Maybe you're right, maybe I am. That's not good, is it? Well, okay, I'll watch that—and for sure I'll broaden my mogul image."

"That's a relief." He watched her bright smile, the light dancing in her eyes while they talked. Beyond her head a burst of purple iris and daylilies colored the edge of the terrace. The whole picture was a portrait he wished he could preserve.

"Mike," she said, more serious now, "tell me about Kendrick Enterprises."

Mike would much rather have talked about the flowers, about her intriguing eyes, about the slow ending of the summer day. "Well, Peggy," he said slowly, trying to shift back to the conversation, "what would you like to know?"

"Anything. Goals, maybe. I mean, what do you want to come of all this? What should Kendrick Enterprises accomplish . . . ultimately, I mean?"

Mike drank his wine slowly, thinking about her question. Evening shadows fell across Peggy's face now, highlighting her cheekbones, the slant of her brows, the lock of hair that wisped across her forehead. It was hard to concentrate when he looked at her, so he looked off into the distance, down the incline toward the lake. The company had plenty of goals, but he didn't think that was what she was asking. They had fiscal goals, purchasing goals, long-range plans for growth and development. He looked back at Peggy and she was still watching him, waiting, oddly wanting some sort of an answer. "Peggy, there are a lot of goals in a company the size of ours, not one single objective. I'm not sure we have an *ultimate* goal."

"I see," she said slowly. "I guess that's true." Her brows pulled together in earnest thought. "Tell me this, Mike, do you ever want to chuck it all, sell all those shopping centers and tall buildings and newspapers, and use the money for good things?"

"The company uses its income for good things."

"Like what?"

"Like paying employees, for example. And we invest some back into the company so it will grow."

"What about the homeless?" she asked abruptly.

Mike frowned. "How did the homeless come into this?"

Peggy bit down on her bottom lip. "I don't know. That was silly of me, I guess. But I was just thinking that making a company grow isn't nearly as important as providing help to people who have nothing."

"Peggy, you're being idealistic. And a little foolish."

"Foolish?" Peggy sat up straighter.

"Sorry, bad choice of words. What I mean is, you don't sell off a company's assets to give it all to the homeless, because then you have nothing left."

"But they have *something*, and—"

"Hey—" Mike stopped her by laying a hand on her arm. Peggy didn't move. "That sounds good in theory, but it wouldn't work at all. For starters, there would be a lot of people out of work if all the Kendrick projects closed down." He looked at her evenly. "Is it the clearing away of those run-down old homes on Whitney that has your dander up? The ones you went down and petitioned for?"

Peggy frowned. "How did you know about that?"

"Every now and then I catch the evening news. I'm not so sure that's a great place to take Billy."

"We were fine," she said, her words clipped and precise. "I certainly wouldn't jeopardize Billy's safety."

Mike removed his arm from her hand and sat back. He watched the anger spark new color in her eyes. Damn, it was lovely. *She* was lovely—naive and idealistic to the point of irritation, but alive and intriguing.

Peggy was standing now. Her body threw a shadow across his lap. Around them tiny pinpricks of light dotted the gardens as the low lawn lights were switched on. "I think I'd better get Billy home," she said.

Mike frowned.

"We didn't intend to stay this long," she said, her words coming out quickly, as if she had to make him understand something.

Mike nodded. He got up and walked beside her into the house. "I'll drive you."

"No, there's no need to do that. The train is fine."

"Don't be silly."

"I'm not silly, Mike."

"Now, wait, Peg." He stopped her in the darkened hallway just inside the door and turned her toward him. "I don't know exactly where the conversation soured, but don't go away angry. My grandmother always told me I should never take anyone's anger to bed with me. Always right those wrongs before nightfall, she said."

"I'm not—"

He tipped her chin up and locked her eyes. "Oh, yes, you are. You think I'm a rich scoundrel right now. I'm really not, Peggy. Not a scoundrel, anyway."

Peggy shivered. His words faded away and her mind attended only to his touch. Each small point of contact created a warm spot on her skin—her chin, her shoulder. She thought if she could look in a mirror there would be pink blotches where his fingers touched her skin. And the warmth didn't stay on the surface but instead melted through her skin, until it ran right through her, coursing through her blood.

Finally she looked up. Her smile was apologetic. "I'm too emotional, Mike, always have been. But I never stay angry longer than sixteen minutes, so your grandmother won't have to worry and you don't have to worry about going to bed."

At that moment, before Mike could tell her how he felt about going to bed, Carmen appeared in the darkened hallway.

"Peggy, there you are," she said and, surprising Peggy, she made no comment at all about finding her standing with Mike in a dark hallway.

"Peggy," she said instead, "Billy is out like a light. I didn't think you'd want to take him home like that on the train. He's getting so big to carry. So Stella called a cab."

"A cab?" Peggy said, her mind trying to visualize the coins in her purse.

"Stella's nephew drives one and it won't cost much. He'll be here any minute. I've got some money—"

"This cab stuff is ridiculous. I'll drive you. It's not that far," Mike said.

But at that moment a horn sounded from the front of the house and Stella called out that Fred, her youngest nephew and a dependable driver if there ever was one, was out in front. They should take their time, she said, his meter was a patient one. Carmen hurried off to collect Billy and his things.

Peggy looked at Mike and laughed. "So much for power, Mr. Kendrick."

He laughed, too, and then walked outside with her.

She stopped beside the car and turned toward him. "This has been a wonderful day. Thank you."

"It's been great for me, too. I don't often come home to activity in the house. It's nice."

Peggy laughed. "Billy is activity, all right." She thanked Stella then, and climbed quickly into the cab after Carmen.

When she rolled down the window to thank Mike again, he was pressing several folded bills into Fred the cabdriver's hand. She opened her mouth to object, but then closed it immediately. She really couldn't object. Fred probably needed the money, and the Lord knew that the only folded thing in her purse right now was a tissue. Her first paycheck from Kendrick Enterprises was still a week away.

Mike leaned over, his hands curling over the window ledge. "I want the three of you to come any time. The pool just sits there. You might as well use it."

Fred gunned the engine.

Peggy spoke over the roar. "That's a shame, and it reminds me that you never answered my question on why you live here all alone."

Mike laughed. "I know you, Peggy, you're filling it up with homeless people, even as we speak…counting the rooms, figuring out how many you can bed down." His tone was light, teasing, and Peggy smiled.

She started to answer, but before the words reached the air Mike had stopped them. Quickly, fleetingly, and right out in front of God and Carmen and Stella and Billy, he kissed her, and then before it completely registered he stepped back, and Fred, the careful driver, squealed out of the driveway on two wheels.

Chapter Six

"I don't know, Casey," Peggy said. The phone was wedged between her shoulder and cheek and with her free hands she was picking up cardboard bricks that Billy had been using to build a house. She tossed them into his playpen, a catchall now for his toys. "Your fix-ups haven't been the most successful times of my life."

"This guy is wonderful, Peg."

"Have you met him?"

"Well, no, not yet, but Pete says good things about him."

"Pete has been wrong before, Casey." She liked Casey's friend Pete, but his taste in blind dates for her seemed too dependent on which client he was trying to woo for his advertising firm.

"No, really, Peg. He is an old friend of Pete's, as well as a client. And Pete adores you, Peggy. So trust him." She paused for a minute, and then spoke again, the tone in her voice indicating she had just had some sort of divine revelation. "Aha, now I get it! I know what it is, Peggy. It's Michael Kendrick, isn't it?"

"What's this big *it,* Case?"

"Peggy, it's me, Casey. I know you. I know that when you forget things the way you have lately, that when you don't mention Billy seventeen times in the conversation, that when you don't—"

"Casey, stop. There isn't anything between me and Mike Kendrick except . . ."

"Yes?" Casey's voice was sweet but heavy in I-told-you-so innuendos.

"Except some sort of a . . . a curiosity. I think it's a case of earthman meets Martian, and we're both curious about how the other operates."

"That's a very odd way to describe a relationship."

"We don't have a relationship. We have a friendship . . . sort of." Mike hadn't kissed her again, even though she had seen him most days since the day they swam at his home. But even though he didn't touch her when they were together, there was something totally baffling between them, something titillating and mysterious. They both felt it, she was sure of that, even though they never talked about it, as if to mention it would destroy the mystery and delight, or perhaps wallop them with the fact of its futility.

"Friendships don't usually bar one from going out on dates," Casey persisted. "I mean, I'd be thrilled if you told me you were seeing Michael Kendrick, but since you say you're not, and since Pete needs a date for this client, a.k.a. *friend,* and since you're not busy tonight and Carmen is free to baby-sit, then why not, Peggy?"

"Oh, all right." Peggy always said all right in the end because it was the easiest way to get off the phone with Casey to attend to Billy's needs. Casey knew it, and Peggy was sure her friend's success in the courtroom was due to this same careful, relentless manner.

"Wonderful. We'll be by at eight."

"I could meet you—"

"Nonsense, I'll have none of your quick-escape devices tonight. See you later, and give Billy a smooch for me."

Peggy hung up the phone and walked into the kitchen to get a glass of ice water. She tiptoed carefully past Billy. It was another record heat day and she had put Billy down for his nap on a giant pillow near an open front window. She drank her water slowly and looked down on him now. An angel. Her life.

The shrill ring of her doorbell made the small boy jerk slightly in sleep, but his eyes remained closed. Peggy hurried to the door.

Two men, dressed in bib overalls, stood in the hallway. Braced between the two of them was an enormous box.

"Where do you want it, lady?" one asked. His cheeks were red and puffy from the exertion of the stairs and Peggy feared for a minute that he was going to collapse.

"Are you okay?" she asked.

"No," he said with difficulty. "No one told us it was a third-story walk-up. What do you have against elevators?"

The second man shifted his hold slightly. "Cut the gab, Harry," he said good-naturedly. "Ma'am, we need to put this down somewhere appropriate, or drop it here in the hall. What's your pleasure?"

Peggy looked from one to the other. "What *is* it?"

"Your order." Harry began edging his way into the house. "The living room or bedroom, most likely. Which'll it be?"

"Which what?" Peggy asked. "Who are you?"

"The lady wants introductions," he said, exasperated.

"Are you Miz Peggy Shilling?" the first man asked. She nodded.

"Then this is your new air-conditioning unit, guaranteed to last a hell of a lot longer than this building. And if you don't mind my saying so, ma'am, you sure as hell need it!" He lifted his shoulder to catch a river of sweat running down the side of his ruddy face.

"I'm sorry," Peggy said, moving aside. "Put it down and rest a minute, but then you'll have to take it back down. There's been a mistake. I didn't order an air conditioner."

The men grunted as they lowered the box to the floor. Then Harry pulled a wrinkled sheet of paper from the large pocket in the front of his overalls. He squinted as he read it. "Peggy Shilling. 441 El Monte. Apartment 3B." He looked up at Peggy.

"That's my address, but—"

"That window over there'd be best," the man said abruptly, pointing to the one large window in the living room. "This here is the top model. It'll cool this apartment and then some. Good choice, lady."

"But I *didn't* choose anything. May I see that?" Peggy took the yellow order form from his hand. It was her address, all right, her name. Just as she was about to protest again, assuring the men that there was no way on God's earth she could begin to pay for a top-of-the-line air conditioner, she saw the billing information. A deep frown furrowed her brow. She looked up at the two men. "Would you wait a minute? Sit down, if you like. I need to make a phone call."

Without hesitation the men collapsed into the two living-room chairs. Peggy hurried into her bedroom. She checked her Rolodex, then dialed quickly. After a brief wait, Mike picked up the phone.

Peggy skipped over the niceties and plunged right in. "Mike," she said, "what's going on here? I can't afford this. I can't afford to pay you back, and I can't accept it. I don't *want* it! What are you doing to me?"

"It's not for you," he said calmly.

"Then tell these two Tarzans to move it!"

"It's for Billy."

Peggy's mouth was open, ready for a retort. She closed it for a minute, then said softly, "I don't remember hearing him ask you for an air conditioner."

"It's not healthy for him in that two-by-four apartment without any air circulating."

"Babies survive far worse."

"Billy shouldn't have to."

He was fighting dirty. Peggy bit down hard on her bottom lip. She frowned.

"You're mad as hell, Peg," he said, "but you'll get over it." He could see her in his mind, biting down on her lip, her brow shadowed.

"I'll pay you back," she said simply, and hung up the phone. He would not do this to her, force this dependence. She wouldn't allow it. He had no right. Her hand was still on the phone and she jumped when it rang again.

"Peggy," Mike said without preamble, "I'm not trying to make you dependent. Only cool. See you soon." And then the phone went dead a second time.

Peggy shook her head and allowed the smile to come. She forked her fingers through her heat-dampened hair and shook her head. Mike. Nice Mike. There he was, a presence in her life. Extraordinary.

CASEY AND PETE PICKED Peggy up promptly at eight.

"You'll love this restaurant, Peg," Pete said as they drove speedily along the highway. "It's *très chic.*"

Peggy laughed. "Great, Pete. That's me, without a doubt."

"We're picking Parker up at his hotel," Casey said.

"Parker?" Peggy repeated, forcing each letter of the name to take on a life of its own.

"He's a great guy, Peg," Pete said. He pulled into the exit lane of the expressway and slowed down slightly.

"Pete, every client of yours is a great guy."

"That's true. But this one even you will approve of. He's buying a company here. Comes from Boston but used to live here. I knew him in high school. You'll like him, I promise."

And for once in his life, Peggy admitted reluctantly, Pete was right. Parker Dunne was smart, funny and a gentleman. And by the time they had had drinks at his hotel and walked down the block to the restaurant, Peggy knew she and Parker would have a great time, maybe even see each other again when he came to town for business, but he would never be more than a DMK, as she called them, the dinner-movie-kiss dates. And that was fine. No entanglements, no fireworks going off, no dependencies. It was funny how all the ideal qualities in the world couldn't set off the fireworks that said, *This is it. This is the man for Peggy.* Funny, she thought, and a damn shame. She really liked Parker Dunne.

"Here we are," Pete said.

Peggy abandoned her thoughts and looked at her surroundings. "Oh, lord," she said in a half whisper.

"Didn't I tell you, Peg?" Pete whispered in her ear. "Chic as all get-out."

At that moment an elegant, gray-haired man walked over to them and, nodding slightly, smiled at Peggy. "Welcome back, Ms. Shilling. It is good to see you again. And how is your son?"

Casey looked at Peggy. Pete frowned. Peggy smiled graciously, then answered the maître d's polite question. When he turned away she lifted one shoulder in a shrug and grinned at Pete and Casey. "What can I say?" she said sweetly, and proceeded to follow the head waiter of Evenings through the elegant hallway and to their table.

As they sat down Casey whispered in Peggy's ear. "Okay, Peggy, tell me the truth. It was Michael Kendrick, wasn't it?"

"No, Casey. That was Simon, the maître d'." She smiled as a waiter appeared and proceeded to place a crisp linen napkin across her lap.

Casey lifted one brow. "I've eaten here twice before, and I wasn't called by name."

"But you're a lawyer, Casey. *No one* remembers lawyers' names."

Pete ordered drinks all around, then grinned at Casey and said, "That's good, because I'm about to change it."

Peggy looked at Casey. Casey was looking at Pete, with the softest look Peggy had ever seen on her earnest, capable, attorney friend's face. "Casey!" she said, her eyes widening.

Casey nodded, her eyes still on Pete.

"Congratulations, you two. What a marvelous surprise," Parker said, and then he motioned for a waiter to bring the best champagne in the house.

Peggy sat still. She felt the tightness in her throat first, and then a sting behind her eyelids. Oh, no, she was going to cry. Right here in the middle of Evenings restaurant.

Casey looked at her friend and squeezed her hand. "Don't, Peg. I knew we shouldn't have told you like this. We didn't intend to, but Pete can't seem to keep his mouth shut."

"I should have known," Peggy said. "I should have been able to tell by looking at you." She swallowed around the lump in her throat. "I'm so happy for you, Casey. For both of you."

"Well, Peg," Casey said, "it's a sign of hope for women everywhere. If a hardened feminist like me can get married, anyone can. Even you."

Peggy laughed through the blur of tears. Casey was her closest friend, her mainstay in those early days of Billy's life with her, her confidante and the one who always managed to calm her down when her emotions ran away with her reason. She felt great joy for Casey, because she knew without question she would be happy with Pete, and she felt a twinge of sadness because she and Pete would no longer have equal dibs on Casey's time. She and Casey would always be friends, but Pete now had the edge.

"I promise not to complain when Casey runs out in the middle of the night to get you out of a jam, Peg," Pete said.

"Thanks, Pete," Peggy said. "I'll hold you to that. And now we need to toast." She picked up the champagne flute the waiter had put down in front of her. "To the most wonderful—"

When her voice broke, Parker, nearly forgotten in the emotion of the moment, picked up the toast. "To Pete and Casey. To a wonderful life. Shalom," he said simply and Peggy smiled at him for his kindness.

They all drank, Pete kissed Casey lovingly on the lips, and then they each accepted a long, elegant menu from the two waiters who hovered over them.

Peggy scanned the entrées and thought of Casey and Pete and marriage. When she had adopted Billy she was so sure she could do it alone. She was bright, capable and certainly had enough love to support him. And she was still sure of her own abilities. But with each new stage in Billy's young life, she became more aware of their twosomeness. The fact that she was absolutely all Billy had sometimes made her sad and a little frightened. She liked watching him with Pete when he and Casey would take them all to Pete's cabin up in Minnesota and Pete would hold Billy up on the back of Fran, his lazy farm horse. And Mike Kendrick...Mike had made Billy grin and laugh. Sure, she could do all that herself, but having another adult there now and then added another dimension to his life. She'd have to think some more about that. She'd have to—

"Peggy?" It was Parker, smiling at her as the waiter stood at her elbow, his eyebrows lifted in anticipation.

"We lost you again, Peg," Casey said, and then she explained the situation to Parker. "This happens sometimes because Peggy usually has twenty-seven projects going at the same time, and she uses quiet moments to sort them out so that each one is a huge success. And it is," she added quietly, smiling at her friend.

"And Casey is known for always coming to my rescue at flustering moments like this and presenting them in the best possible light," Peggy said. She looked up at the waiter. "I'll have whatever Parker is having," she said, and resolved silently to concentrate on the evening and the pleasant man who would be paying for her very expensive meal.

The biggest surprise of the evening came at the same time as the dessert, a lemon-liquor concoction that melted in Peggy's mouth. Peggy was listening to Parker comment on how he enjoyed trips back to Chicago when out of the corner of her eye she saw a large, familiar-looking hand grasp her companion's shoulder.

"I'll be damned—Parker Dunne!" said a deep, familiar voice.

Peggy's head snapped back. Her mouth fell open.

"Michael Kendrick!" Parker shoved out his chair and stood. He was smiling broadly. "I don't believe it!"

"It's great to see you, Parker. What are you doing here?"

It wasn't until Parker had explained his trip that Michael looked around the table at the others. His eyes stopped when he came to Peggy, and the polite smile the others received turned broader, warmer. "Peggy!" And then he frowned slightly and glanced at Parker.

"You know each other?" Now Parker was talking, and Peggy was glad because she wasn't sure where her voice had gone. The shock wasn't from seeing Mike at the restaurant; it wasn't even the fact that Mike knew Parker, her date.

It was, she admitted to herself later, the gorgeous, sophisticated, exquisitely dressed brunette who was standing just one step behind Mike.

"Sure I know her," Michael was saying. "Peggy works for me." Peggy winced. *Peggy works for me.* Not Peggy's my friend; or I've taken Peggy out to dinner; or she's fallen asleep in my pool; or I've kissed her in front of the cabdriver. But Peggy works for me. And she did. And that was, after all, what it all came down to.

"Well, you're damned lucky, Kendrick, just as you always were," Parker said, and then the two made the other introductions—Casey and Pete and the elegant woman named Melanie Hudson, Michael's date.

Melanie smiled graciously and shook hands, then paused when she looked at Peggy. "Have we met? You look very familiar."

"I don't think so," Peggy said, forcing a smile. "I'm sure I would have remembered."

"No," Melanie insisted, "I have seen you before. Recently. In Michael's office, perhaps?" The way she said "Michael's office" made Peggy shiver. It was proprietary, intimate.

Peggy shook her head no. She would have remembered this woman if she had met her. No, they had never met, Peggy was certain of that.

Melanie was still looking at her, her head tilted to one side, and Peggy squirmed beneath the scrutiny but didn't know how to escape it, so she lifted her chin, looked at Mike and smiled.

Mike smiled back, a slightly crooked smile. His eyes were laughing now. He was wondering how long Melanie would pursue this. She was incredible with faces and names, but Mike knew where she had seen Peggy, and he also knew there was no way she would figure it out. She'd never connect this beautiful, poised woman sitting at a table in Evenings restaurant with the woman handing out leaflets in blue jeans and a T-shirt with a baby strapped to her back. She looked about as much like a protester tonight as Melanie herself.

"Well," Melanie said at last, "it will come to me eventually. I never forget a face." She smiled then, graciously, and suggested to Michael that their friends would probably be wondering where they were if they didn't get to their table soon.

Michael shook hands all around and after a few more words to Parker he followed Melanie across the room. Peggy watched them until they disappeared from sight.

For a moment there was silence at the round table. And then everyone spoke at once.

"He seems like a nice guy," Pete said.

"Kendrick will never change," said Parker.

And Casey leaned over and whispered, "Peggy, he's even more gorgeous than I remember!"

Parker Dunne was smiling. "It was great seeing him. I haven't seen Michael in years. He was one hell of a tennis player."

"And equally as successful in business," Pete said. "His company is one of Chicago's largest and most successful, and the bulk of the expansion has happened since Michael joined his father."

"Doesn't surprise me," Parker said. "Kendrick was one of those golden guys that was successful at anything he tried. You work for him, Peggy?"

"Kind of. It's a temporary job, nothing important." And then she changed the subject and took a drink of her champagne in an attempt to wash away the discomforting feelings that were threatening to engulf her. Those twittering, heart-lurching feelings had come back the instant she'd seen Mike's hand on Parker's shoulder. His *hand,* for heaven's sake. What was going on here? Whatever it was, it was rattling, disconcerting. And Peggy didn't like not feeling totally in touch with what was going on inside her.

When the evening ended and Parker Dunne walked her up the three flights to her apartment while Casey and Pete waited in the car, she felt calmer, but the unruly feelings were still there at the fringes of her consciousness.

Parker stood for a minute beside her, looking down into her eyes. "He's gotten to you, hasn't he?"

"Who?"

"Kendrick. I've seen it before."

"He hasn't gotten to me. I work for him, that's all."

Parker leaned over, kissed her lightly on the lips and smiled at her. "Peggy, you're a wonderful lady. I like you a lot. Be careful. Michael is one of the best, but the Kendricks are a force unto themselves."

"Parker—"

"I'm sorry if I'm speaking out of turn," he said. "I like you, that's all. I'll call you next time I come to town and see how you're doing."

Peggy smiled. "That would be nice. And I'll be happy to tell you I'm doing just fine."

She lifted herself on her toes and kissed him again, a light, brief, thank-you kind of kiss and then he was gone.

"WELL, PEGGY, what do you think?"

Peggy and Joe sat in the cool studio and sipped dark, old coffee as the flickering images of the first cut of the documentary on havens for battered women played across the screen.

"I think you need to be more forceful about this, Joe. It's good—great filming—but it's so...so deodorized."

Joe laughed. "You mean it smells?"

"No. I mean you've covered over some of the really rough spots, prettied them up."

"Peg, this is a commissioned documentary. It's to be used by charity groups to help raise money."

"So show them what the money is really going for. You had some emotional clips of real abuses, but they were cut."

Joe looked over at her. "Peg, you're probably right. But, sad as it may seem, they don't want to see that. There are limits to what ladies will watch at a luncheon while they're eating chicken salad."

Peggy frowned. "It's a cop-out, Joe. You need to move out of your life a little."

"Move out of my life?"

"Yes. You people who have been raised on nannies and summer camps and Harvard need to—"

Joe was laughing now. "Hey, Peggy, calm down. Is this a tirade against the rich, or what? What's this *you people?*"

She shook her head. She didn't know what had gotten into her. She hadn't slept well, maybe that was it. And then the morning had been hectic. After Billy was settled with Carmen she had rushed over to Children's Hospital to work with the clown troupe, then skipped lunch and hurried to meet Joe at the scheduled time. She sighed. "I'm really sorry, Joe. I'm tired, that's all. I don't begrudge you your privilege, it's just—"

"Hold on, Peggy. For starters, although I don't think this has much to do with anything, I grew up in south Chicago in a two-bedroom frame house with a roof that leaked most of the time. I went to Harvard because I filled its quota of smart midwestern kids without money and I got a full ride. But something else is bugging you. What is this about?''

"I thought...because of your friendship with Mike—''

"You underestimate the boss man if you think he picks friends by their pocketbooks, Peggy.''

"I'm sorry, Joe, no, of course I didn't mean that. I just assumed, I mean you and Mike—''

"Are close friends because we like and respect each other. It has nothing to do with where or how we were raised. I didn't have money when I was young. I have lots of it now, but what difference does it make?''

"None. Absolutely none. I'm sorry I got into all this, Joe.'' She paused, then looked up at him, her head tilted to one side. "But I still think you need to take some of the cosmetics off this film. Come on, let's look at it again.''

When Mike arrived an hour later Peggy and Joe were so intent on the film they didn't see him standing at the back of the studio. He stood there quietly, watching them in the dimly lit room. Peggy was gesturing, her voice rising and falling, and Joe was jotting down things on a yellow pad, nodding occasionally.

They worked well together, Joe and Peggy. And he could tell from watching them that Joe respected Peggy's opinion, even though he didn't always agree. He couldn't see Peggy's face fully from where he was standing, but he could see her profile and the flush that covered her high cheekbones. There was something so terribly alive about her, and he found being around her was exciting.

Seeing her Saturday night at Evenings had been a surprise. It had startled him at first, and then, later, vaguely bothered him, although he couldn't put reason to the feeling. Nor could he rationalize why thoughts of her had stayed with him for the rest of the night, through the long dinner, the dessert and the perfunctory, unsatisfying, good-night ritual with Melanie. And then the three days that followed, although he hadn't seen Peggy, she had been there in the middle of his thoughts, her laughter brushing against him like a butterfly wing.

He walked across the room now, pushing aside the confusion and concentrating instead on the warmth created by a room holding two good friends. "Hey, you two," he said, his long strides bringing him to their side. "Anything I can do to help?"

"Oh, sure, the big man comes when the work is all done," said Joe.

"The only way," said Mike. "Could you two use a drink to end the day?"

"Not me," said Peggy. She was busy shoving her notes into a plastic briefcase. "I have a very important date—"

"With Parker Dunne?" Mike asked. The question slipped out without thought. Damn, why had he asked that? Who Peggy Shilling's big dates were was no concern of his.

A few seconds of silence, as long as the shadows of dusk, stretched across the room. It wasn't the question that heated the air but the feelings that accompanied it. Peggy frowned. Now she knew what had bothered her all morning. It was the same thing she sensed in the tone of Mike's question. She had been attacking a life-style, giving Joe a terrible time with her misplaced aggression, because she was jealous—jealous of the gorgeous Melanie Hudson.

Jealous! Peggy had never been jealous of anyone. And the slight edge to Mike's words held the exact same feeling, echoed the uncomfortable emotion that had nagged her then. She smiled slightly. She was jealous of Melanie Hudson; Mike was jealous of Parker Dunne. And neither of them had any reason or *right* to such feelings. It was funny, really, ludicrous, how such uninvited, unfounded feelings could creep inside one. Her smile broadened until she noticed both Mike and Joe were looking at her curiously.

"Oh, sorry," she said. "Who is my big date? My big date is William David Shilling."

"Oh," said Mike. He released the air he was holding in his lungs unknowingly and grinned. "Well, that's tough competition."

"You betcha it is," said Peggy. She laughed.

"Tomorrow, then. Tomorrow we can have a drink—maybe a drink and dinner would be better—and you two can fill me in on how everything is going."

Peggy looked at Joe, who nodded.

"Sure," she said. "Tomorrow."

And as she walked to the bus stop she wondered how, if Mike Kendrick was this solicitous of wining and dining all his company's several thousand employees, he managed to stay so fit.

The thought made her whole body smile.

THE BUS WAS LATE and crowded, but not even the noises and odors of hard-working people on a hot summer's day could dampen Peggy's spirits. And her heart was still light as she flew up the stairs to her apartment. She felt like dancing, singing, scooping Billy up in her arms and waltzing around the apartment.

"Hello, my little love, I'm home," she called out as she flew inside.

"I guess the *little* eliminates me," a deep voice said.

Mike sat in the chair, his body leaning slightly forward, and Billy was firmly implanted on his knee. His leg was moving rhythmically up and down and a huge cowboy hat on Billy's head bounced to the movement.

"What..." Peggy whispered. "But how...?"

"This here's cowboy Bill," Mike said, nodding gravely toward Billy. "Carmen disappeared across the hall to get ready for a hot date."

"I just saw you."

"Good. You remembered." He grinned. "Looks like I beat you home. By the time I had my car out of the garage, you were nowhere to be seen or I would have given you a lift."

"I would have asked for one but I didn't know you were coming here."

Mike's knee picked up a cantering speed. His large hands splayed out, encompassing Billy's waist to hold him in place. "I didn't really know it myself. Damn car just sort of drove itself here."

"I see."

"It did make one stop, though."

"Where was that?"

Mike nodded toward a huge picnic basket that was on the floor near the door. "When I called ahead from the car, Carmen said she didn't think you and Billy had any specific plans for tonight, so I stopped and got some food. Picnic stuff. It's a great night for it."

Peggy walked over and lifted one half of the lid. Tantalizing odors floated up. She thought the smells were squeezing her heart until she realized she had stopped breathing.

"It's good food. You'll like it," Mike said.

Peggy turned and walked back toward Mike. She lifted Billy off his leg and kissed him soundly on the cheek. He grinned and wrapped his arms around her neck. "Horsey," he said clearly.

Peggy nodded. "Horsey."

Billy squirmed out of her arms and toddled back to Mike and his waiting saddle.

"Mike, are you sure you have the time for this?" She knew as she spoke that the question was inadequate. Time wasn't what she was wondering about. It was far more complicated than that.

"I'm here, aren't I?" Mike said. "And I'm not exactly known for being places against my will." His disarming smile prevented her from saying more, or from protesting his presence.

Besides, the protestations would be awfully weak. Mike Kendrick wasn't at all bad to come home to.

PEGGY PICKED THE PARK. Mike had suggested one on the north shore, not far from his house, but she had insisted they stay in her own neighborhood.

The park was a green, rolling haven in the middle of the bustling, congested and slightly run-down area, and it even had a shell for the amateur orchestra that was playing that night.

"This is great, Peg," Mike said as they wove their way through the labyrinth of worn blankets to an open spot near a large tree. He was pushing Billy's stroller with one hand and carrying the picnic basket with the other.

"Billy likes the music and all the people," Peggy said. She began to unfold the blanket on the grass while Mike set down the basket of food and lifted Billy from his seat. "The orchestra plays mostly show tunes, easy-to-listen-to kinds of things, and sometimes they have a polka band that fills in."

Mike settled himself on the blanket, stretching his long legs in front of him and lining his back up against the trunk of the huge cottonwood tree. He had planned on working late tonight, reviewing some new contracts for a shopping center in Santa Fe. But something had taken hold of him, some new, bizarre voice in his head, and without reasoning it out he had listened to it and headed for Peggy's house. The picnic idea came to him as he passed a new gourmet food take-out on Michigan Avenue. *Picnic* seemed to merge nicely with the images of Peggy that floated in and out of his orderly mind.

He wouldn't admit to her that his own experience with picnics was slightly different. He vaguely remembered a birthday party he had had. Seven years old? Eight? His mother had thought a picnic was the perfect motif for that age, so she had had tables set up across the sprawling lawns, covered them with brightly colored linen cloths and ordered an all-American meal of crisp fried chicken and all the trappings. Ponies were brought in for treks around the estate, the kids were given kites and Frisbees and squirt guns and, since baseball seemed to go along with the wholesome theme, his father had pushed buttons, called in favors, and most of the Chicago White Sox baseball team had shown up to play with the kids and give them autographed balls and bats. The ballplayers had even stuck around to watch the sky light up with the party's grand finale, a dazzling fireworks display.

"What are you smiling about, Mike?" Peggy asked.

"I was just remembering the last time I was at a picnic," he said.

"Was it as nice as this?"

"Nope," he said. "Not even close."

LATER, AFTER A DINNER of lemon-basil chicken, pasta salad and the chocolate cake that decorated Billy from his forehead to the toes of his tennis shoes, they all played on the swings and merry-go-round—Mike pushing Peggy, who held Billy tightly in her lap—and then, finally, they flopped down together on the blanket in satisfied weariness to listen to the strains of Cole Porter drift up into the black summer sky. Billy, quiet at last, curled up between them, his head on Peggy's stomach as he nursed a bottle of apple juice. His heavy eyelids drooped and before the orchestra had completed "Begin the Beguine," he was sound asleep.

Mike smiled and half closed his eyes. His back was against the tree and his arm was looped comfortably around Peggy's shoulders, cushioning her head. Half of him listened to the music while half attended to the enormous sense of satisfaction that washed through him.

Peggy shifted and looked up into his face. "Are you comparing picnics again?" she asked.

"Nope, I'm not comparing anything at all. I'm just enjoying, that's all."

"Do you like this?"

He nodded.

"Do you . . . does . . ."

"Do does," Mike said. "Sounds like an old song."

"Does Melanie like this sort of thing?" She forced a lightness into her voice and the words came out sounding like someone else's.

"Melanie," Mike said carefully. "I guess you mean Melanie Hudson, the woman with whom I was dining—"

"When you introduced me as your employee. That night."

Mike chuckled. "It's nuts, Peggy. I'm not a game player when it comes to women, honest. But running into you with Parker Dunne bugged me. I tried to keep the smile, the charm going, but frankly, I was irritated."

"Tell me about it. I'm not that way, either, Mike. And I know we don't owe each other explanations, but when I saw that tall, slender beauty on your arm I wanted to spill my dessert down the middle of her exquisite gown.''

"Crazy," said Mike.

"Dumb," said Peggy.

Mike's voice grew soft and serious then. "Melanie is an old friend," he said. "Our families are also friends. And that's really all it is. At one time maybe it could have been more, but it would have been a matter of convenience more than anything else. I'm not quite sure why yet, but it's important to me that you know that, and that you know there are no other Melanies in my life."

Peggy smiled. That was certainly fair. She leaned into his shoulder.

A light wind began to rustle the trees then, rippling blankets and sending loose sandwich wraps scuttling across the green lawns. The sounds of the music floated on the breeze, now louder, then softer as the wind carried the notes.

Mike felt a soft tickle on his cheek and opened his eyes. All around him were fluffy white flakes, bits of down settling on the blanket, on his legs and arms and dotting the green grass around them.

Peggy smiled. "Summer snow," she said. "It's late this year."

"Summer snow," Mike mused. It was a perfect name, he thought, for the delicate covering of the earth with tufts of seeds floating off the cottonwood trees.

"We had a huge cottonwood tree at home," Peggy was saying, "and every year—in May or early June usually—it snowed for us. I remember the first time I noticed it. I thought it was a miracle. I looked outside and the earth was covered with snow on a beautiful seventy-degree day. I called to my mother to come and see the summer snow."

"Nice," Mike said. He rubbed a fluff of silky cotton between his fingers. "Summer snow...a miracle..." The image captured something intangible growing inside him. Soothing coolness in the midst of heat. Fire and ice. He played with it, turning it over in his mind, and it captured something he couldn't put a name to. It was the magic of Peggy, he decided, the magic of summer snow.

He tucked the image away into the folds of his mind, knowing it meant something significant to him, although at that moment he didn't want to analyze it too closely for fear of damaging its young life. He would let the feeling that came with the image grow on its own.

Later, when a local singer with an extraordinary voice belted out "I've Got You Under My Skin," it seemed natural for Mike to draw Peggy closer and trail his fingers lightly along the tender skin of her neck. And when Peggy shivered and smiled, and he kissed the top of her head, it was expected. When she turned her head, lifting her chin slightly so she could see into his deep blue eyes, Peggy knew Mike would kiss her on her lips, a tender kiss, familiar and willful and carrying a promise that this was somehow more than a passing in the night, a chance kiss on a black velvet summer night, a night of summer snow.

Peggy responded from a hidden well deep down inside her that brought tears to her eyes and a life to her soul that she had never missed because she had never known such feelings before.

And between them, his small body curled like a question mark, his thumb now replacing the bottle of apple juice, Billy slept soundly.

Chapter Seven

Peggy awoke early the next morning. She walked dreamily into the kitchen, plugged in the coffeepot and looked out into another hot, sunny day. But her mind didn't notice the heat and humidity or the fact that her window was cracked and the screen needed repair. All she saw was the brightness, the bending vinca vine and soft blue periwinkle in the flower box outside her window. She stretched and smiled and thought about the evening in the park. *Evening in the park*. The phrase sounded as romantic as she had felt. As romantic as she *still* felt.

The ardor of the night before had been tempered and controlled by a sleeping eighteen-month-old boy, but Peggy was as sure as she'd ever been of anything in her life that every ounce of desire she had felt for Mike had been reciprocated.

But where would it go from here? Maybe Mike would wake up and think better about the whole thing and she'd find herself without a job. No, even if he came to his senses and realized a romantic rendezvous with Peggy was ridiculous, he wouldn't take away her job; he was far too kind for that.

The phone rang and scattered her thoughts across the kitchen. She lifted the receiver.

"Who wrote 'Peg o' My Heart'?" Mike asked before she could say hello.

"Darned if I know." Peggy smiled.

"It's a nice song."

The silence that traveled across the phone lines was an easy one. Peggy was sure she could feel him smiling.

"Well, that's about it for now," Mike said. "And Peg...?"

"Hmm?"

"Thanks for last night."

He hung up then and left Peggy feeling as warm as the yellow sunshine flooding her small kitchen.

Billy padded in on bare feet, reminding Peggy she had a day to begin. She scooped him up, whirled him across the room and plopped him into his high chair for cereal and a banana.

It was going to be a busy day. She had a clown clinic in the morning with some college kids who were apprenticing during their summer vacations, and in the afternoon she was scheduled to work with Joe and go over some editing. And then dinner... Mike had said he wanted to have a business dinner with her and Joe. Not bad, not bad at all. Everything she had to do all day long would be a pleasure... and some of the pleasures she was even getting paid for!

"Know what, Billy?" she said, moving close to the high chair. "You have one lucky mom!"

Billy grinned and shoved the last half of his banana into her pocket.

MIKE HAD SLEPT WELL, better than he had in a long time. His life was a rat race, but usually he thrived on it. Maybe it was that he never stopped long enough to let it seep in that relaxing actually was pleasurable. Maybe it was the damn genes; he was like his father in so many ways. He got a thrill out of watching the company grow. There was real satisfaction in seeing the figures mushroom, watching new ventures pay off. It was in his blood and there was no denying it. But the pleasure he derived from being in Peggy's company was a new thing, a brand-new pleasure that surprised and invigorated him.

Summer snow, he thought. His face relaxed into a smile. Yeah, that was it.

THE DAY FLEW BY FOR PEGGY. The workshop in the morning was an enormous success. The college kids were fresh and enthusiastic and would be wonderful with the children. And as a bonus, they would all be around to help with a benefit that the clown troupe would be participating in to help Children's Hospital.

That finished, she had rushed down to the studio to meet with Joe and the crew where the documentary was shaping up beautifully. When they finally turned off the machines and walked out of the studio, Peggy was tired but happy and looking forward to her second wind and the dinner ahead.

"I guess we're still on for dinner tonight, Joe?" she said as they walked into the cool hallway.

"As far as I know," Joe said, then glanced at his watch. "Mike will probably be in the front office right now, waiting for us. Mike is a man of his word and he never forgets."

They turned the corner and there was Mike in the foyer, just as Joe had predicted. Peggy's heart made a strange lurch when she saw him. Then she noticed the woman with long black hair standing at his side. She stood tall and confident, talking to Mike, her long fingers punctuating certain words, her face calm and composed. It was another Melanie. Peggy cringed.

Joe strode immediately over to the woman. "Hi, Nancy," he said. "Peg, come and meet a friend of ours. Nancy Spaulding, Peggy Shilling. Peggy is helping me on a documentary," he explained to the woman.

Peggy smiled. Joe had kissed the woman on the cheek and the action made her irrationally happy. She shook the woman's hand and pleasantries were exchanged. Nancy was friendly but guarded. Peggy had the feeling she was being checked out completely.

"Can you join us?" Joe asked.

Nancy smiled at Joe. "No, darling. Actually, I've come to kidnap you. There's a cocktail party for that project I told you about. Somehow there was a miscommunication regarding the date, so I didn't have a chance to tell you sooner. Anyway, I need a date for it. You'll come, won't you?"

Mike spoke up. "We can have the business catch-up tomorrow, Joe. It works out better for me, anyway." He looked at Peggy. "Okay with you, Peg?"

Peggy nodded, trying to hide her disappointment. And then she chided herself. It was silly to look forward to a business dinner. Now she could get home early, spend some time with Billy, get some grocery shopping done.

The small group conversed for a few minutes longer and then Nancy and Joe left.

"Well, I suppose I ought to be going, too," Peggy said.

"Oh, no, Peg, you need to come with me. I need an escort, too."

"But—"

"I had accepted a dinner invitation for tonight but I kind of forgot about it when I asked you and Joe to meet with me."

Mike noticed Peggy's slow smile.

"What?"

"Oh, nothing, except Joe just finished telling me that you never forget commitments. Looks like Joe was wrong."

Mike was silent for a minute. He finally gave Peggy a lopsided grin. "Joe's right. I never do forget commitments and I feel downright silly about this. It slipped right by me and I don't know how. Seems I haven't been as clear thinking the past few days as I am normally. Must be the weather, do you think? Maybe it's all that summer snow." He watched the slight blush creep up Peggy's neck.

She shifted from one foot to another, then smiled and looked him in the eye. "Well," she said, "it's not a problem, anyway. Now you're free."

"And you are, too. So please come with me?"

"Come with you where?"

"To my house. My *family's* home, that is."

"Your family's house?" Peggy croaked.

"Sure. There's always enough food for a dozen ex-tra. My mother doesn't believe in letting the cook skimp."

"But I'm a stranger, Mike. You can't just invite a stranger home like that—"

Her words were stopped by the look on his face, the slightly sexy lifting of his brow, the half smile that turned her knees to jelly.

"Okay, so we're not strangers."

"Not in my mind. And if you kiss strangers the way you kissed me last night, woman, you'd better watch—"

Peggy put her hand out to stop his words. "Okay," she said quickly. "So we're not strangers, but we're not close friends, either. I mean not *old* friends, the bring-home-for-dinner kind."

"In my mind I've known you a long time, Peggy."

"Minds don't count, only calendars."

"Come on, Peggy, it will make it far more pleasant for me if you come. You'll be a welcome addition. Mother always enjoys meeting new people, and you've already met my father."

Peggy threw her hands into the air. "My point ex-actly!" The words came out with such fervor that both Peggy and Mike laughed. She put one hand on Mike's arm. "I mean, a stranger would be better than me, Mike. Admit it. I'm not your father's favorite per-son."

"He won't even remember."

Peggy tilted her head to one side and looked at him. "You're saying I'm easily forgotten?"

"I'm saying my father remembers the gross national product, the fiscal accountability of all his vendors and the exchange rate in seventeen countries, but not young women he bumps into once on a crowded street."

"Mike, that's fine for you to say, but I don't think it's a good idea." She paused, and that, she thought later, was the fatal mistake, that single, innocent pause. Because that was when Mike took her by the elbow and steered her through the heavy glass doors and to his car.

PEGGY TRIED TO KEEP her mouth from dropping down to her waist when they drove through the wide portico-guarded gates to the Kendrick family home. She nearly succeeded, but all her fine intentions were blown away when they passed the initial stand of stately pines and she saw the house.

"Good God almighty," Peggy breathed, her eyes the size of saucers.

"This is it," Mike said matter-of-factly.

"It's... it's big."

"You could say that. I guess it is a little big for two people."

"It's too big for twenty people. Thirty. Fifty!"

Mike pulled his car up near the front of the house, parking in the wide paved circle driveway. Peggy slipped out of the car and leaned back against the door, her eyes scanning the panorama in front of her. It was a three-storied, vine-covered mansion, complete with a tower that was made out of stone and circled its way up to the clouds.

Mike followed her gaze. "You know," he said, "as a kid I never noticed its size much, maybe because there were huge chunks of it we didn't really use."

Peggy just stared. She had seen large houses but she had never seen anything as lavish as the Kendrick home. "I can understand not using all of it. You could house half of Chicago's homeless in the left wing alone."

Mike laughed. "I don't think my mother would go for that. She likes to do things for the homeless as long as she doesn't have to see them."

"She could probably pull that off here, too," Peggy mused. Then she paused and shifted her gaze from the house to Mike. "I'm sorry, Mike. I don't mean to sound flippant. I've no right. Your parents probably worked hard for what they have."

"Yes, they did. But your point about the size of this place is legitimate. The only way I can justify it is that it keeps a whole lot of people in jobs—gardeners, cooks, maids, painters. And that's worth something."

"Of course it is. That's worth a lot."

"It wasn't until I left home that I realized it was rather peculiar to have more employees living on the property than actual family."

"Well, it's a beautiful place," Peggy said now, her voice hushed. She was looking off to the side, to the bright summer flower beds that edged the parklike setting, the tennis courts just visible beyond the trees, the ponds and terraced green lawns. Everything was leafy, lush and magnificent. "It's like a movie set."

"Actually, it was used in a movie once. But never again. It drove my mother crazy to have all those muscled grips and cameramen walking on her flowers."

"I guess if I had flowers like that I'd want to protect them, too."

"Enough about flowers. You can't eat them. Let's go on in."

Peggy looked startled, as if she had planned all along to eat dinner off the hood of Mike's car. Then she shook her head, laughed into the fading sunset and said, "Of course. Let's go in."

An exceedingly formal butler led them into the library. As she looked up at the man's stiff neck and rod-straight back, Peggy felt an incredible urge to giggle. This was too much, too theatrical. In fact, the scene they were playing would probably be panned by critics as too stereotyped.

"His name's not Jeeves, is it?" she whispered to Mike.

"Walter," Mike said and they both laughed softly.

The library was quietly elegant, filled with leather-bound books and a portion of Mr. Kendrick's impressive art collection. French doors on the far side of the room looked out onto a wide terrace and as Peggy moved closer she caught glimpses of Lake Michigan and a yacht harbor.

At the sound of footsteps, clipped and light, Peggy turned from the windows. At that moment Claire Frances Kendrick came into the room. Mike's mother didn't walk into a room. She *entered* a room, a stage-like entrance, and commanded her surroundings by her presence. She wasn't a tall woman, about as tall as herself, Peggy judged, but height was irrelevant. Her piercing dark eyes and carriage made her seem six feet tall.

"Michael, dear," the Kendrick matriarch said, her words filling the room like a pontifical blessing. Long, perfectly manicured fingers touched each of her son's shoulders while Mrs. Kendrick kissed him on his cheek.

"Mother," Mike said easily, "I'd like you to meet a friend of mine. This is Peggy Shilling." After kissing him, his mother had taken a half step back, a kind of dance step, Peggy thought, and she didn't seem to have noticed Peggy until Mike spoke. At his words she pivoted toward her, looked at her very carefully, then smiled graciously and extended her hand. "It's lovely to meet you, Miss Shilling."

Her voice was perfectly controlled, her words perfect, and Peggy wanted to turn and walk out of the house never to come back. But of course she wouldn't—this was Mike's mother, after all. And if Peggy let herself be intimidated, that was her problem, not Mike's or his mother's. And with a resolve *not* to be intimidated, Peggy smiled brightly at Mrs. Kendrick, shook her hand firmly and told her what a pleasure it was to meet her, as well. "And please," she added, almost as an afterthought, "please call me Peggy."

"Certainly, Peggy," said Michael's mother. "Now shall we all go out on the veranda? The others are already here."

Peggy looked quickly at Mike. *Others?* her eyes asked.

Mike grinned and took her by the elbow, leading her behind his mother to the flagstone patio beyond.

A small group was gathered at the far end, seated on cushioned chaises and looking out over a magnificent pool. Mr. Kendrick stood as they approached. The sun was in his eyes and he squinted as they walked closer.

"R.J.," his wife said, "Michael is here with his guest."

All eyes focused then on Peggy. "Ah," Mr. Kendrick said, his face expressionless.

"This is Peggy Shilling," Claire Kendrick was saying.

"We've met," her husband answered.

Peggy shot another quick glance at Mike. So much for his father's selective memory.

"Miss Shilling and I ran into each other one day," Mr. Kendrick said. His tone was solemn.

Peggy searched his face for a sign of humor. Was he being funny? She couldn't tell. His face was still, inflexible. All right, if he wouldn't tell her what he meant, she'd interpret it any way she pleased. And it pleased her, although she wasn't at all sure it was the truth, to think he had a sense of humor. She smiled broadly at him, her clear green eyes meeting his blue-black stare directly. "We did, at that," she said cheerfully, "and neither of us looks any worse for wear. It's nice to see you again, Mr. Kendrick."

R. J. Kendrick didn't speak but Peggy thought she saw an inkling of a smile behind his cigar. When she looked again it was gone and she wondered if it had been wishful thinking on her part.

Mike's mother was now introducing her to a small, elderly woman. She was sitting next to Mike's father. She was so small and folded up that Peggy hadn't seen her at first, but when she looked at her now she wondered how she could have missed her. The woman was old—late eighties, Peggy guessed—but she had the loveliest, liveliest eyes Peggy had ever seen. She immediately moved toward her, taking her pale, veined hand in her own.

"Mother Kendrick," Claire was saying, "this is Michael's employee, Peggy."

The old woman smiled warmly at Peggy. "So you are Peggy. Michael has told me about you." She glanced up at Claire Kendrick and said, "Peggy is not just an employee, Claire. She is Michael's friend." Then the elderly woman shifted on the outdoor couch and patted the empty space next to her. Peggy gratefully sat down.

The last introduction was to Elizabeth Kendrick Barton, Mike's older sister. She was a younger version of her mother—elegant, imperious and perfect. Peggy unconsciously moved closer to Mike's grandmother.

"Now, Peggy, you are a business associate of Michael's, I understand?"

"A business associate?" Peggy laughed lightly and sipped the champagne she had been poured. "Well, I suppose I am, after a fashion."

"Peggy is a consultant on a film Joe is producing," Mike added. "It's the one about the Family Haven group."

"And how is that coming?" asked R.J.

"Joe says it's looking good, and he claims Peggy has a lot to do with that."

"How do you come by this particular expertise, Peggy?" Claire asked.

"I discovered the group when a friend needed the services they offered," Peggy said.

"A friend?" Claire said. Her brows had lifted slightly, carefully.

Peggy nodded. "They literally saved her life. And then when a social service agency I do some writing for wanted to help them get a grant, they asked me to work on it."

"You're a writer?" Elizabeth said.

Peggy took another drink of her champagne. Why wasn't Mike changing the conversation? She didn't want to talk about herself. She smiled at Elizabeth. "I like to write, but I'm more a jack-of-all-trades. I do anything that will pay the rent and feed Billy."

Mike cleared his throat and broke the silence that followed Peggy's enthusiastic description of her work. Then he said, "Billy is Peggy's little boy."

Claire Kendrick stifled a slight cough. She was sitting forward now and Peggy could feel her intense examination even without looking at her. It was so strong, so sharp, so *measuring*. "I see," she said.

Peggy couldn't tell from her tone whether she thought she was a murderer or a prostitute. Maybe both. No one asked further about Billy and Peggy was at first relieved, then curious about it. It was unusual, since in the year and a half she had been mothering Billy she had found people to be very interested both in him and in the details of raising an eighteen-month-old as a single parent. But the Kendricks didn't seem to be at all inquisitive about such matters.

She felt a small pressure on her arm and looked over at Mike's grandmother. Her hand was resting lightly above Peggy's wrist. "Peggy, I do like your looks, yes I do," she said. "You and I must talk some more, but not on an empty stomach." She lifted one thin finger into the air and said, "Claire, isn't it high time we had some food?"

"I agree, Grams," said Mike. "Both about Peggy's looks and about dinner. I'm starved." And at that moment, as if on cue, Walter came out to tell them that dinner was now served in the dining room.

The dining room was cool and fragrant. Peggy breathed in the lovely smells and headed toward the seat next to Mike. But Claire Kendrick stopped her midstream.

"Peggy," she said, "you will sit next to Mr. Kendrick." A chair on the opposite side of the table was pulled out for her by a young man in a white jacket, and Peggy sat down.

Elizabeth sat next to Peggy, Grams next to Mike and Claire and R.J. sat at the table's ends.

"Peggy, my dear," said Grams, "did you know I used to be a dancer?"

Peggy thought she heard Mike's mother sigh, but when she looked in her direction she had a small, polite smile on her face and was picking up her spoon to begin eating the cold soup that had been placed on the table.

"A dancer? Fascinating. That's great, Mrs. Kendrick," Peggy said.

"Now, dear, you are to call me Grams. Nearly everyone does."

Peggy smiled. "Thank you, Grams. And I'm not surprised you were a dancer. You're still very graceful."

Grams patted her hand. "You are certainly a dear, sweet child. Michael told me I would like you."

Peggy wondered when this conversation between Grams and Mike had taken place, or why, but of course she didn't ask. Instead she told Claire Kendrick how lovely the chilled soup was, took a sip of the cold white wine that had been poured for her and asked Grams where she had danced.

"A revue in Toledo, Ohio," Grams declared proudly. "And I was the lead dancer before I left to marry Robert senior. Should never have given it up, but at the time, you see, it seemed the right thing." Her voice drifted off a little, but when she focused back on Peggy, her eyes were bright and clear. "It was before women's lib, you understand."

"Ridiculous, mother," R.J. Kendrick said. "You were always a women's liberation advocate." He hadn't said much during the early part of the evening but Peggy noticed that he spoke now with noticeable affection in his voice and manner. He went on, smiling at his mother. "You never needed a movement to form your attitudes, at least not that I can remember."

The others at the table laughed. "Yes," Mike said, "Grams has always been a trailblazer."

"And we love her for it," said Elizabeth.

Well, good, Peggy thought. We all have something in common, our affection for this wonderful gray-haired lady. At least that's something.

"I wish I could have seen you dance," Peggy said.

"Well, I shall certainly show you pictures, Peggy," she said.

"That's a great idea, Grams," Michael said. "I'd like to see them again, too."

Grams's eyes lit up. She turned to Peggy. "Now and again Michael takes me dancing. He cuts a pretty good rug himself although I'm so terribly slow now."

Claire then began telling them about a series of big band appearances that would be held in the fall at the Drake Hotel and Peggy escaped into the lovely image of Mike and this captivating, frail, gray-haired lady dancing together across a polished ballroom floor. She could see it clearly in her mind's eye, Mike's strong, muscled arms supporting the diminutive Grams, her eyes shining and her tiny feet barely touching the floor as he moved her to the music. Nice, she thought, very nice.

Two uniformed maids came in to collect the soup bowls, and Peggy half listened to the conversations going on around her. Mike and his father were discussing an upcoming board meeting now, and Claire was explaining to the rest of them the details of a planned trip to the Orient. Peggy sipped her wine quietly and watched them all, the gathered Kendrick family. She liked Grams a lot. Elizabeth was very re-

served—polite, but not terribly friendly, and Mr.
Kendrick, for all his gruffness, didn't frighten Peggy
anymore. But Mrs. Kendrick was an enigma. Her
proper social facade was so perfect that Peggy couldn't
see beyond it. She allowed the waiter to refill her glass
of wine, then leaned slightly forward, trying to concentrate on the conversation.

A young woman, somewhat younger than Peggy,
wedged her body between Peggy and Elizabeth in an
attempt to remove the soup bowl. Peggy sat back to
accommodate her and then, for reasons she couldn't
later explain, she looked up into the young maid's
face.

Her mouth dropped open. "Max!" she exclaimed,
her voice rising above the subdued voices and the
hushed movements in the room. "Max, it's you!"

The maid's brows shot up into her long bangs. "Oh,
my God, Pegs!" Her eyes were as round as a full
moon.

In an instant Peggy had pushed back her chair,
stood and thrown her arms around the young woman
with the soup bowl.

Max dropped the bowl onto the table and hugged
Peggy tightly. Soup splashed onto the linen table-
cloth.

"What the hell—" R.J. muttered. Claire stared silently at the activity, her long face disturbed.

"Peggy! I don't believe it!" squealed the maid.

It was the subsequent silence that pulled Peggy away
from the young woman. She took a step backward and
her eyes sought Mike. "Mike," she said, her voice
lifting with excitement, "this is my cousin Max. My

aunt Bessie's daughter. Maxine. Lord, I haven't seen her in so long. Can you believe this?'' Her face was flushed, her eyes sparkling.

Grams looked up, beaming. "What a lovely happenstance,'' she said.

Claire, who had half risen from her chair, sat back down. "The maid is your cousin?'' Lovely shaped brows lifted on her expressionless face.

"My *favorite* cousin,'' Peggy said, brushing a stray lock of hair from Maxie's cheek. "I can't believe it. How is your pop, Maxie? And when on earth did you come to Chicago? No one told me— Lord, this is such a wonderful surprise.''

When she looked around the table for confirmation, Peggy saw that, in fact, it was a surprise, a walloping surprise. Mike's mother was frowning now, a frown just slight enough to reprimand, subdued enough to still be gracious. Elizabeth looked smug, a we-should-have-known look on her face. R.J. looked irritated and hungry. This was interrupting his meal and the only thing privileged enough to do that involved money. Certainly lost cousins didn't count. And Grams, lovely Grams, was bathed in grins. She was thoroughly enjoying herself.

Mike stood, walked around the table and shook Max's hand warmly. "Well, hello, Maxine,'' he said. "I'm delighted to meet you. This is a great coincidence. You resemble Peggy a little.''

"Same crazy laugh,'' Maxie said, and followed it up with a sampling.

"I used to baby-sit for Maxie when she was a baby,'' Peggy said. She looked back at her cousin and beamed. "This is wonderful, running into you like this. You're going to have to come over and meet my Billy."

"Mom told me you had a baby. That's great, Pegs!"

"He's so beautiful, Maxie. You'll love him. Wait, I have a picture—" She looked around for a minute, and then looked back to Maxie with regret. "No, I don't. I didn't bring my purse. But you'll see him in person soon enough."

"Oh, I hope so! I've only been in the city for a couple of weeks or I would have tracked you down."

"Where are you living?"

Maxie laughed. "Oh, a little dump near the University of Chicago, but it's cheap and I can get to summer classes easily."

"Maxie, that's terrific!" Peggy hugged her again. "Oh, I'm so proud of you."

Mike stood on the sidelines watching the two women. Maxie's laughter came as readily as Peggy's, unrestrained and lifting. It was refreshing and honest. A little bit of human drama, played out right there in the staid Kendrick dining room. Maybe the walls would hold it, soak it in and retain it. Neither Peggy nor Maxie were the least bit self-conscious, and maybe that fact delighted him the most. He looked over at Grams, and although she probably couldn't hear half of the excited conversation passing between the two women, she was, nevertheless, enjoying it all completely.

R. J. Kendrick cleared his throat then, and with
such momentum that Peggy and her cousin jumped.
The others seemed accustomed to the noise.

"Clearly this is a wonderful surprise for you two
young women," R.J. said, his thick white brows
nearly touching one another, "but if you don't mind,
perhaps we could eat our dinner now and continue this
reunion at another time? I'm sure Max...ah, Maxine has duties to which she must attend."

Maxie blushed and Peggy laughed softly. "I'm
sorry, Mr. Kendrick. We got a little carried away. The
Shilling clan is known for that."

"You should see us at *real* family reunions," Maxie
added and then the two laughed again and this time
Grams laughed along with them and clapped her
hands. "Wonderful, wonderful," she said, her thin
lips resting then in a satisfied smile.

"This is so strange," Peggy said, "you serving me
dinner like this, Max." She slipped back down on her
chair, her eyes lingering affectionately on Maxie's
face.

"Crazy," said Maxie.

"Imagine," sighed Claire Kendrick.

"My kind of show," said Grams.

WHEN MIKE TOOK PEGGY HOME a few hours later, the
sky was clear and black and filled with stars.

Peggy sneaked a look at Mike as he maneuvered the
car through the winding streets of the exclusive sub-
urb. His strong jaw was relaxed, his eyes aimed
straight ahead and his thoughts somewhere far away.
Peggy couldn't tell at all what was playing itself out

inside his head. While she watched, Mike's lips moved, shaped into a smile, and he lifted one hand from the wheel and settled it on her shoulder. It rested there for a minute and then with strong, blunt fingers he began to massage the tender skin just behind her neck.

Peggy sighed in pleasure.

"You're a little tense."

"I always get that way when I leave the lion's den."

Mike's laughter was low and soothing to her. "It wasn't that bad, was it?" he asked. "I thought you were great."

"In what sense?"

"In handling the situation." His smile was broader now.

"Ha." She gave a short laugh. "Was I great when Maxie started telling me about Uncle Harry's trouble with the law and accidentally dropped the pie down Elizabeth's back?"

"Elizabeth needs to loosen up a little. Max handled the situation fine, I thought. Her apology was sincere, and she even offered to cover the cost of cleaning."

"Oh, Maxie wasn't handling anything. Max was being Max. She was probably oblivious that there *was* a situation." Peggy's voice grew softer. "She's great. I love Maxie."

"She feels the same about you, that was obvious."

Peggy nodded her head and her hair brushed against his hand. "I hope your father's indigestion goes away."

"My father's indigestion doesn't have anything to do with you."

"Well, that's debatable."

"Grams loved the whole evening."

Peggy laughed. "I know. She's wonderful, Mike."

"She's her own person, that's for sure. She has some bad days now, off and on, but on her good days she's someone to be reckoned with. You ought to hear her when she gets mad. Grams's vocabulary is part trial lawyer, part sailor."

Peggy laughed. "You're close to your grandmother?"

"Yep. She's a gem."

"Mike—" Peggy imposed a silence that would command his attention.

He looked over at her once, then said, "What, Peg? What's on your mind?"

"Why did you invite me there tonight?"

Mike was silent for so long Peggy was beginning to regret asking the question. Finally he shook his head. "I don't know for sure. It happened without a lot of thought. But in the long run I think I wanted to take you there because that's all a part of me. And I wanted you to see it all. It seemed important somehow."

They were driving along the lake and every now and then the houses fell back, the road took a dip and they could see the water off to the side. The lake was immense in its blackness and the moon's light falling on it magnified the sight. Peggy fell into the wonder of the night and the confusion of Mike's words, and barely noticed when the car took a turn off the main road and pulled into a long rectangular overlook on a slight bluff above the waters of the lake. "Where are we?" she asked.

"This is a north shore make-out spot. It's called Lovers' Lookout."

"Do kids still make out?"

Mike nodded over to the far end of the graveled area. A lone yellow car, its back end rocking slightly, was parked at the edge of the guardrail.

Peggy laughed.

Mike's fingers played lightly along the skin of her neck. Each small movement sent rivers of delight running through her body and she basked in the pleasure of it all. "Do you come here often, big boy?" she asked finally. Her voice was husky and her head leaned back into the crook of his arm so she could see up into his face.

"Not for many, many years," he said. Then he laughed softly. "The last time was in my father's new Porsche. I 'borrowed' it, but forgot to mention it to him. We—there were several of us—came up here to razz the guys who had brought girls. Give them trouble. We'd sneak up behind the parked cars and stand on the fenders, rock the cars, that kind of silly prank. But that night we managed to ruin everyone's night, ours and those who had come up for loftier purposes. My father had reported the car stolen. It never occurred to him that his son would stoop to such underhanded theatrics. So he called out the highway patrol and there were spinning lights and noises over short-wave radios and booming voices everywhere. They surrounded the place. It was great."

Peggy chuckled. "Did you ever come here for, ah, 'loftier purposes' yourself?" she asked.

"Once."

"When?"

Mike paused for just a second, then he looked at Peggy. "Tonight," he said.

When he smiled at her it was with such tenderness that Peggy could barely breathe.

"Ah, tonight," she said, and the words came out in a kind of sigh.

"Yep." He tugged on a lock of her hair. "I don't know what the hell this is all about, Peggy, but there's something going on here. Has been for some time now."

In the dim light of the moon she tried to read his face, his eyes. "Maybe it's the moonlight," she offered.

"Maybe it doesn't need analysis right now," Mike said. "Maybe it just needs a little affirmation."

"Affirmation," she whispered. Her head felt light, filled with tiny shocks of anticipation and pleasure. Filled with desire for Mike Kendrick.

"Like this," Mike said then, and when he lowered his head Peggy was waiting. His lips pressed down eagerly on hers and she welcomed the hungry thrust of his tongue.

She felt the dam burst; she was a bird set free, all the things Carmen quoted her constantly from the romance books she devoured in between psychology texts.

"Oh, Peggy...." Her name was a half whisper gathered in his throat.

She pressed closer to him, wrapping her arms around his neck and meeting the plunge of his tongue with the tip of her own, darting together, exploring the dark, moist caves.

Mike dug his fingers into her hair, holding her head immobile while he drank in her kisses and let the desire build within him. She had this power over him—incredible and intense and remarkable.

He moved his hands down her shoulders, over the silky-smooth skin of her bare arms, and then slipped his fingers beneath the buttons of her blouse until he felt the warm skin of her breasts.

Peggy gasped. Each place he touched he left a mark, a hot, delicious finger of pleasure. She felt her breasts harden beneath his touch, her nipples stiffen until the pleasure approached pain.

"Oh, Mike," she breathed, her breath and the single word sliding across his hot cheek. She pushed her hands through his hair, her heart pounding furiously.

He was kissing her throat now, his tongue leaving a moist trail down its hollow, his lips dipping lower until her blouse fell open and they found the heated skin of her breasts.

Peggy's fingers twisted uncontrollably in his hair, seeking an anchor that was not to be found.

At first she thought the rocking was her heart, that incredible swooping motion, up and down. Mike, too, ignored it as a part of the emotion sweeping them both into some land beyond reality.

But then the laughter reached her ears, strangers' giggles, smothered noises, and when she lifted her head and looked back over Mike's shoulder she knew it wasn't her heart or her passion.

It was three teenagers bouncing on the rear fender of the car, three kids out for a night of mischief and wreaking havoc on Lovers' Lookout.

She looked at Mike.

His face was flushed with desire, his eyes slightly glazed. Slowly they focused and he managed a lopsided grin. "My grandmother always warned me about this," he said, his voice still husky.

Peggy began to grin. "What?"

"What goes around, comes around. Yeah, that's it. Damned if I ever knew what it meant before."

And then they fell into each other's arms, their building, manic laughter driving the youths away from the car and on to better, more interesting receptions.

Chapter Eight

At first Peggy felt as if she was back in high school, swallowing the teachings of the black-robed nuns. The boys bouncing on the back of Mike's car had been guardian angels, sent to protect her and keep her within the boundaries of the formula for good, decent girls.

But when she calmed down enough to look at the situation, her confusion had nothing to do with nuns or limits or angels, nothing at all. It had to do with her, with Peggy Shilling and Mike Kendrick. Maybe it was Casey getting married that had her in such a state. Maybe...

She had never been the kind of woman who dreamed of the house and picket fence and husband. She might have had that dream once and somewhere along the way it was shattered by her own family life, but in her adult life it wasn't something she gave a lot of thought to. She *did* give thought to avoiding the life her mother had had—being overly dependent on a man, and then having your life shattered, taking to drink, the way her mother had done when her father died. Sandra Shilling couldn't even pay a bill herself, call a plumber, get a job. No, Peggy would never be that way, never allow a man to dominate her, to tell her how to think and feel, and to leave her in pieces when he was no longer around to hold her together. Peggy would hold herself together. And Billy, too.

But those thoughts and the feelings she had for Mike Kendrick didn't fit in the same basket. Mike sent her head spinning, her heart soaring, and she couldn't think about anything logical or reasonable. All she could think about was the way he made her feel, the lovely sunshine he brought into her days.

She walked out onto the fire escape and watched the faint streaks of dawn begin to appear in the eastern sky. It was another hot day and the heat seemed to paint a soft, hazy sheen across the dawn.

Peggy had managed a couple of hours of restless, unsatisfying sleep before she finally gave up, got up and plugged in the coffeepot.

Her mind was a mess. She had never wanted a man the way she had wanted Mike Kendrick last night. Every fiber of her being had screamed out for him, pleaded with him to become a part of her, to complete her in some crazy, mystical way. She had thought she wouldn't survive it, the pulling apart of their bodies when the kids had intervened, the gentle, passionate kiss when he had dropped her off at her apartment.

But there was Billy to consider. How did it all fit together, the ragged pieces of this damnable puzzle?

Her thoughts were so loud, so invasive, that she barely heard the phone, and she only managed to get it on the seventh or eighth ring. A persistent caller, her mind registered vaguely. And then, more clearly, it registered that it was five o'clock in the morning and under normal circumstances people didn't call other people at five o'clock in the morning.

Her voice shook as she said hello.

"I know it's early, but I knew you'd be up."

"How...how did you know that?" Her knees were weak and she slid her back down along the wall until she sat on the floor.

"I was out on the veranda watching the sun come up," Mike was saying, "and it occurred to me that you were up, too, standing at your kitchen window or out on the fire escape watching it with me. I could feel it."

Peggy shivered.

"So I called. I hope I didn't wake Billy."

"It takes far more than a phone call to wake Billy."

"Was I right about the sunrise?"

"Yes, you were right," she said quietly. "It's beautiful."

"Doubly so when shared."

Peggy nodded and Mike seemed to hear. His voice grew thoughtful. "Peg, last night was hard on both of us."

"Yes."

"Peggy—"

"Mike—"

Their names collided, fusing together into one, and Peggy felt a tug inside her, an instinctive tightening in her loins. *Lord, I'm crazy,* she thought, squeezing her eyes shut and her knees together as she pressed her back to the wall. *I'm nuts, a basket case, loony-tunes.*

"It's okay, Peggy," Mike's voice soothed her.

"No, it's not. It's lust, Mike. That's not okay."

Mike laughed softly. "It's not lust, darlin'. It's a lot better than lust."

There was a moment of silence but Peggy felt him so intensely, even in the quiet. The faint sound of his breath across the lines fell on her cheek, heated it.

"Peg, I have some land up in Wisconsin that I need to check on."

"Land?" she said faintly, her mind trying to change course.

"Yes. It's not far from here, a few hours' drive at the most. I'd like to go up later tonight, early evening, check things out tomorrow, and then come back to the city tomorrow night."

"I see." But she didn't see. He had no commitment to her. He didn't need to explain his absence. He shouldn't feel that responsibility.

"Mike—" she started, but he continued.

"Peg, I want you to come with me."

Her heart began its erratic journey.

"If Carmen can't stay with Billy, I have someone lined up."

"No!" she said instantly. "I don't leave Billy with strangers."

"Of course you don't," he said calmly. "I meant Stella, my housekeeper. Stella isn't a stranger. She's very fond of Billy and she loves kids."

"Stella..." She said the name but only to fill the silence. The issue had become a baby-sitter for Billy, but she still hadn't dealt with the invitation. He was asking her to go away with him. For the night.

My Prince Charming   149

"Peggy, I know this is all scaring you a little. God knows the feeling is something new to me, too. All I'm asking you to do is get away from the city with me, and away from the fact that you work for me, that you're not nuts about my family—all those things that can cause confusion. I want to get to know you better in a more . . . more pure kind of setting."

She laughed softly at his choice of words. Pure. This was pure, going away together for the night? What would the nuns think? "Pure," she repeated.

Mike laughed, and then his tone grew serious. "Peggy, I'm not asking anything of you. There's a great old inn near the property where we can stay. They have cabins with lots of rooms. You can have five or six of your own if you want. I'll sleep on the beach, in a field, on a different floor, whatever you want. I just want to be with you."

His voice was so gentle that she thought she was going to cry. Damn, why would she cry? She had always been so in charge of her feelings but lately . . . lately she seemed on the verge of tears or laughter most of the time.

Mike's voice went on, soothing, stroking. "I know it's probably hard for you to be away from Billy overnight, but we can call frequently—there's a phone in the car—and maybe it will be good for you, and for Billy, too."

She knew that was true. She had talked to Casey about it recently, about not wanting to be obsessive, about how hard it was, since she was everything to Billy—and he to her. And the authors of all Carmen's child psychology texts concurred.

"So, Peg o' my heart," Mike said on the other end of the line, "will you come with me?"

PEGGY DIDN'T KNOW HOW she had gotten through the day. She didn't even know if she had actually given Mike an answer, but she did know she was going with him. She knew *that* because she couldn't eat all day and her head was spinning, and she kept forgetting her phone number. Her fellow clowns at SMILE teased her gently about it that afternoon as they got ready to visit their young patients at Children's Hospital.

"Peggy, you're flushed," said Stacia Stanley, a middle-aged woman who was one of Peggy's favorite partners when the clown troupe went out. "Are you sick?"

"Mentally, maybe," Peggy answered, then followed it up with a laugh and quickly covered up her natural flush with a blob of red makeup that circled her cheek.

"Aha," Stacia said. "I was that kind of flushed once."

"What happened?"

"I married him."

Peggy didn't answer. Instead she dipped her fingers into a pot of brilliant orange cream and with exaggerated concentration, applied it to her face.

CARMEN WAS ONLY TOO EAGER to stay with Billy, so Mike picked Peggy up at five at her own apartment and in minutes they were soaring along the highway, headed north.

He had kissed Peggy lightly when they got into the car, then whisked her off. And he had brought tapes to play—Peter Gabriel, James Taylor, some soft jazz, and the music provided a comfortable backdrop for her thoughts.

Mike was in no rush for serious conversation. He sat at ease, his elbow resting on the window ledge, his strong fingers guiding the steering wheel. Peggy glanced at him every now and then and he seemed to feel the glances and would smile her way, sometimes squeezing her knee or her shoulder. The gestures, his nearness, all made her crazy. Crazy and content at once, and filled with wonderful tinglings.

As the sky began to darken, Peggy realized she was hungry but she didn't want to break the lovely mood so she pushed it away and instead listened to the music, to the hum of the car and to the strange new sounds of her heart.

After a while they turned off the straight highway and took to country roads, narrow two-lane roads on which Mike's green Saab and the occasional Ford pickup truck vied for dominance. They drove up and down rolling hills and passed neat farms with cows grazing lazily in the meadows. They drove through a town with one grocery store, one hardware store, one tavern and a diner with the day's menu written on a chalkboard in the window.

"Where are we?" Peggy asked.

"Almost in heaven," Mike answered. "Wait, you'll see."

A short while later a smattering of weathered gray signs announcing fresh bait, groceries and boat rent-

als appeared along the side of the road. Now she at
least knew that, wherever they were, it was near water. And then, as the car followed the hilly road lined
with feathery pine trees, she caught glimpses of it—a
clear, blue, tranquil lake.

"Here we are," Mike said finally, and he slowed the
car, then turned into a graveled driveway. It curved
down through the trees toward the lake and to a rustic inn. The inn was nestled in between the pine trees
and the lake spread out behind it. Peggy stuck her
head out the window and breathed in the scent of pine
and freshly mowed grass, of lake life and timber and
fresh fish grilled on hot coals.

"This is Timber Lodge," Mike said. "It's also
known as 'almost heaven.' I've stayed here for years
when I've come up for business or just to get away."

Peggy slipped out of the car.

"What do you think?" Mike asked.

He was standing in the driveway, his hands shoved
in his jeans pockets, his eyes focusing beyond the inn
to the lake. There was only a smattering of light left,
and it outlined the trees on the other side of the lake,
creating a hauntingly beautiful silhouette.

Peggy felt a lump grow in her throat. It was wonderful.

Mike wrapped an arm around her shoulders and
walked her into the inn. He had never brought anyone to this inn before, never shared the place to which
he escaped when the business world was threatening to
take over his life and he needed a breather. He had
never *wanted* to bring anyone here. Until now. "I
knew you'd like it," he said to Peggy.

The inn was rustic and the accommodations Mike had made for them were luxurious and considerate—a cabin with two suites set apart from the rest of the inn in a sweet-smelling grove of ash trees and lilac bushes.

Peggy sat on a wicker chaise on the freshly painted porch and looked out over the lake. A glass of chilled champagne sat on the table beside her. "Why do I always feel I'm dreaming when I'm with you?" she asked. "This is magnificent, Mike, a magnificent dream."

"Magnificent isn't what I want, Pegs. I want you to like being here. With me."

She looked over at him and smiled. "That's what's magnificent," she said.

LATER, HAND IN HAND, they walked back over to the inn for a late dinner. The cozy dining room was nearly empty but when they sat together in a bay window, their table lit by an old lantern, it didn't matter. If it had been full it would have seemed empty to them.

There were a few lights dotting the lake, probably small fishing boats, Mike explained, "or maybe a couple of lovers finding a private spot, who knows." He clinked his wineglass against hers and took a drink.

Peggy looked again at the lake. "Almost heaven," he had said about this place, and she felt he was right. The feeling that trickled through her, warming her bones, fogging her mind, wasn't earthly, that much she knew. She focused back on Mike and smiled over the rim of her glass. "Tell me about this place."

"Not much to tell, really. It's a family place. Most of the people are from Chicago or Milwaukee, people who avoid the crowds in Michigan and come here instead. The same people come back year after year and those who own summer homes pass them along to children and grandchildren. The whole place is a carefully guarded secret. The lake doesn't even have a name because people feel it'll be more protected that way."

"It must be called something."

"It is. It's called Paradise Lake by those in the know. The fellows who make maps and the surveyors call it Number twenty-seven."

Peggy laughed. "Does your family vacation here?"

Mike shook his head. "This place is a little, well..."

"Rustic," Peggy offered.

"Kind of. They have a place up in Michigan at Harbor Point where most of their friends summer. But I've always liked it here. I've been coming up here since I was a kid. Our company has some property and developments in the area and I'd tag along after my father when he came up to check on them. He used to take me fishing on the lake sometimes."

Mike paused and looked out the window as he climbed into years past. After a minute he went on. "Those were probably some of my best childhood memories. Certainly the only ones of my father doing something just with me."

"I'd love to bring Billy to a place like this sometime."

"When he's a little older he'd probably like to fish out here." Mike smiled then, touched her hand lightly and ordered them each the house special—fresh trout lightly sautéed with almonds.

The waitress was discreet and no one hurried them as they sat for an hour over the peach cobbler dessert, their heads slightly inclined toward one another, their hands meeting now and then on the checkered table-cloth.

By the time they headed back to their cabin the grounds of the inn were silent except for night sounds—the scurrying of small animals in the woods, an occasional bird calling to a mate and the gentle lap of water against the sandy shores of Paradise Lake. They walked over soft, spongy beds of pine needles and their steps released a clean, pungent smell that made Peggy feel slightly heady. She was acutely, al-most painfully, aware of Mike's presence beside her. "I think the odor of pine needles is an aphrodisiac," she said softly.

There was a lot more going on than an aphrodisiac at work, Mike thought. He'd wondered briefly on the drive up whether he'd made a huge mistake. What was he asking of this woman? Mike was known for his cool-headed business decisions, his savvy and sure mind. But this decision hadn't been made with his head at all. Peggy Shilling did something to him that no other woman had been able to do. She blurred his sixth sense; she messed up his thinking process. She made him feel things deep in his gut but they denied rational analysis. He held his head back and looked up through the branches into the vast black sky. And then he pulled Peggy closer to him and hurried along the path.

When they got back to the cabin they stood outside on the porch, breathing in the clean lovely air. Mike left for a minute, then returned with two tiny thimble glasses of an orange-flavored liqueur. It wasn't until Peggy took it from him that she realized her hand was shaking. A small trickle of fear had run through her when Mike left her side, a forewarning, a last-ditch effort by her childhood conscience. But the alternative—telling Mike that maybe this was a mistake, perhaps they should go back to the city because there wasn't any way she could spend the night in the cabin without being with him—*that* alternative was absolutely unthinkable.

She looked up at Mike, smiled and leaned into his side. They sipped their drinks in silence, their minds and bodies wrapped in the majesty of the night and of each other. Peggy felt only a small tingle of nervousness, hardly enough to attend to.

But it disappeared completely when Mike turned her slowly toward him and kissed her. It was a slow, familiar, wonderful kiss and Peggy slipped her cordial glass onto the wicker porch table and responded hungrily.

"I'm going to have to bottle pine needle scent," Mike murmured. His voice was a soft breath on her neck.

"We'd be millionaires."

"We could call it the Scent of Paradise," Mike said in between tiny nibbles on her neck.

Peggy moaned.

"You okay?"

She shook her head. "I'll never be okay again. My legs are Jell-O. What did you do? There's no support left. My whole skeleton structure has disappeared."

Mike rubbed two fingers beneath the curve of her breast. "Not entirely," he said.

Peggy's heart clattered wildly beneath her chest.

Mike felt its beat and smiled.

She looked up at him and thought she would burst. Behind his head was the black sky and an enormous moon, smiling, offering some sort of benediction. A perfect night. A perfect man.... She ran her fingers down the sides of his face, down his chest, then slid them beneath his knit shirt and rubbed her palms across the flat of his stomach.

Mike took in a quick gulp of air. "Peggy, watch it—" he managed. "I...don't know...if you...know..."

She smiled, her eyes looking directly into his, into the desire that was gathered there. "I know," she said.

He cupped her head and held it still. "What do you know?"

"I know you wasted your money on the extra suite," she said simply, and she took his hand and led him inside.

Mike had left a light on in the downstairs bedroom and it lured them now like a lighthouse beacon.

When they reached the door to the bedroom Mike paused and Peggy looked up at him, her eyes bright with desire. She pressed two fingers to his lips.

"Shh. Yes, I know what I'm doing." Her voice was low and trembling. "I don't feel pressured, Mike. I didn't know on the way up here how I'd feel, but I knew my heart would tell me. It did."

"Hearts can sometimes mess you up."

"Not this one." She lifted his hand and pressed it to her heart. "This one is pretty dependable."

Mike looked down at her. She had closed her eyes and there was a small smile on her lips waiting to be kissed.

He did, with all the pent-up emotion of weeks now, weeks of wanting Peggy. He kissed her eyelids, her cheeks, her lips, and the shiverings he felt beneath his lips only made him want more.

"The legs," Peggy whispered. "They're giving in again."

"Can't let that happen," Mike said, and scooped her up in his arms as easily as lifting a doll.

She looked up at him and traced his mouth with the tip of her finger. "Not bad transportation if you can afford it."

"Can you?" he asked huskily, and began to walk through the shadowy room to the wide bed.

"I don't know, Mike," she said against his chest. A single flicker of fear passed through her, and then was banished. "But for tonight, this joy, being with you, is right. No matter what happens later, no matter what."

He laid her gently on top of the quilt. "You've messed up my thinking, Peg, but there's one thing I know for sure." He pushed her hair back from her cheek, then rubbed it gently with the curve of his fingers. "I would never hurt you, Peggy. Never."

Peggy's heart was swelling, her pulse racing; she could barely keep from reaching out and pulling Mike to her. She needed his closeness, his touch. A sudden spring of tears collected in the corners of her eyes and she blinked them away, nodding her head against the pillows. "I know that, Mike," she said.

Mike reached over and flicked off the bedside light and the room was suddenly bathed in thin white moonlight. It spread across the bed like honey, covering Peggy's still form.

Mike balanced himself, a hand on each side of her, and leaned over her quiet form. "Peg o' my heart" was all he said. And then he began to trail kisses down her throat and across her collarbone, hot, hungry kisses that made Peggy squirm. He tugged her blouse loose from the band of her skirt and pulled it up, exposing her breasts. Slowly, gently, his fingers massaged the silky skin, and then he bent low once more and his mouth kissed her breast tenderly.

"Oh, Mike," she breathed, and the words floated back to her ears from some faraway place, some place toward which she knew she was heading and couldn't wait to arrive.

Mike stood then and his movement left cool air washing over her heated skin. She opened her eyes and looked up to see him standing beside the bed in a patch of moonlight, stripping off his clothes. She had dreamed about seeing him this way, fantasized about his broad, solid chest and the dark hair that shadowed it, touched in her dreams the muscles that shaped it. But her fantasies had tricked her; reality was far more magnificent. Mike's lean, tan body was beyond dreaming, and the reality of it sent shivers up and down her body.

"Is the lady watching me?" he asked, his eyes meeting hers. "Not fair unless we're on equal footing." He walked two steps back to the bed, his long, well-built body casting shadows across her form. And then, in swift, sure movements, he slipped off the rest of her clothes and left them in a pile on the floor.

The moonlight made her look like a carved statue, a collection of beautiful curves with lights and shadows playing across the alabaster beauty of her body. His breath caught in his throat and he felt a tightening inside himself.

Peggy lay quietly beneath his gaze but she could feel it, warm and caressing on her skin, and it sent a rippling river of desire coursing through her.

Standing there, Mike could see her body react, could see the tightening, the slight shifting of her hips. But what squeezed his heart and made his breathing difficult was the light that danced in her eyes and the love he saw there.

"Peggy—" he whispered. His voice was hoarse, unfamiliar.

"Mike, don't say anything. Just come to me." She held her arms up, inviting him into her bed, and he slid down beside her, burying his head in her breasts. "Oh, Peggy," he whispered, his breath hot against her flesh. He felt as if he'd come home.

When he lifted his head she was looking at him, her green eyes filled with desire. "I've never felt quite like this before, Mike. You've . . . you've done something crazy here, and you'd better handle it."

He lifted himself on one elbow and looked down into her sweet smile, her dancing eyes. "You're a lot to handle, Peggy." His fingers trailed along her breasts, circled her nipples.

She squirmed. Her voice was ragged when she spoke. "I . . . think . . . I *do* think . . . that you're up to the task, Kendrick."

"You think so?" He rubbed his palm across her abdomen. "We'll have to see, won't we?"

Peggy reached up, her hands circling his broad shoulders, tugging him to her, and he came, readily and willingly and unable to stay apart any longer.

His body slid over hers gently and Peggy urged him down, closer, until his chest was against her breasts, the whole length of their bodies touching, connected.

When she opened her eyes, Peggy thought the room was filled with stars. She lifted her head to kiss him, her teeth nipping at him, her tongue tracing the edge of his lips until he moaned in pleasure.

"Oh, my darling," Peggy said. "Do you know—"

Mike moved inside her then and her words broke off as she began spinning to crazy heights, up to catch the stars that floated above her. Higher and higher until in a moment of perfect joy she and Mike cried out together and caught the brightest star in the night.

THEY AWOKE HOURS LATER, tangled in each other's arms. Peggy brushed Mike's hair away from his eyes. "I want to see what you look like now, after . . ."

The room was still dark, the moon their only beacon. Its light fell across Mike's smile. It was that boyish smile that belied his power and money. It was the smile Peggy loved. Her heart swelled.

He touched her lips with the tip of his finger. "I'll never look the same after you, Peg," he said.

She rubbed her palms over his chest, her fingers tangling in the dark springy hairs. Then she leaned over and dusted his chest with kisses.

Mike's breath caught. He felt the urgency in his body, the sudden, incredible, dizzying desire that had propelled him through the night.

"Incredible, isn't it?" she murmured against his chest, feeling his desire. "Do you think it can get any better?"

Mike turned toward Peggy, his body lining up against hers. He kissed her lips, her throat. "Hmm, I don't know, darlin', but there's only one way I know to find out..."

And they did.

Chapter Nine

Peggy woke up to cool breezes and clear sunshine—
and an empty space beside her in the wide bed. She
looked around, her eyes slowly adjusting to the
morning light. *Almost heaven,* she thought. Yes, Mike
was right. That's exactly where she was.

Her mind filled with lovely images and she looked
slowly around the room. A small clock on the bedside
table told her it was shortly after seven. She stretched
and smiled and listened for noises but the only sound
she heard was the gentle lap of water against the dock
and an occasional bird.

"Mike?" she called out softly, and then she laughed
at herself. Why was she whispering? Did she not want
anyone to know she was there? No, that wasn't the
way she felt at all. She didn't care if the whole world
knew she was there. The incredible joy that filled her
had to be good; such joy should be shared.

She slipped out of bed, stretched again and realized
how good she felt. Every bit of her, every muscle and
fiber and whatever else made up her crazy body, felt
marvelously good. But mostly her heart felt good.

Light and happy and full. She began to hum as she
slipped on a robe and wandered through the cabin. A
pot of coffee was brewing in the kitchen and two heavy
mugs were set out side by side, but there was no Mike.
Not in the living room, nor in the suite on the upper
floor.

Peggy frowned. "Mike?" she called again, louder
this time, but still there was no answer.

She went back to the kitchen and filled one of the
cups half full of coffee, half milk, then walked out to
the front porch and settled herself on a swing that
hung from the ceiling. She tucked her feet up beneath
her and sipped her coffee, gazing out over the blue-
green lake. It was quiet this morning; a small boat was
tethered to a dock below the cabin and a lone fisher-
man sat nearly asleep just offshore, but there was no
Mike, not for as far as she could see.

She had spotted his car through the bedroom window, so she knew he couldn't have gone very far. Who
knows, she thought, maybe Mike was a runner, up at
five to get in a few miles before breakfast. That would
certainly explain the marvelous strength in his limbs.
Or maybe he meditated, did Zen, went to church every
morning! A flood of possibilities enveloped her, along
with the realization that she had no idea what Mike did
in the morning. And that was just the beginning of the
things she didn't know about Mike. Here she had gone
off to the country with a man she barely knew.

But the thought wouldn't stick because her heart
knew Mike Kendrick, and her body knew him now,
and what he did at seven o'clock in the morning didn't
matter a tinker's damn.

A soft breeze rustled the leaves of a giant elm tree shading the porch and stirred Peggy's hair. She rested her head back against the swing and closed her eyes. A feeling of great contentment came over her and she sighed softly.

Mike found her in the same spot an hour later, sound asleep. He set the box of cinnamon rolls on the table and laid the wildflowers lightly across her legs. She was sitting sideways, one arm curled behind her head on the back of the swing and her knees up, her feet tucked beneath her. She had a soft smile on her face. Beside her, on a small table, was a half-empty cup of coffee.

She moved slightly and the white robe covering her knees fell apart, revealing a slice of skin.

Mike shoved his hands into his pockets and stood there, daring himself to be still, to refrain from touching her, from taking her into his arms and loving her. Watching her was something all in itself. He saw a vulnerability in her while she slept, a kind of delicacy that had been blurred in the passion of their lovemaking. Seeing it now stirred him in new ways and he fixed his jaw, fought against the tightness in his loins.

He had awakened early and gone for a run, a luxury he didn't often have at home. He knew if he stayed in the bed next to Peggy for longer than five minutes, he wouldn't be able to leave her alone. So he'd slipped on a T-shirt and shorts and hit the road. On the way he had passed a small country bakery and picked up the homemade pastries. The wildflowers had been offered by a wizened old woman who was just opening her roadside stand. They were what Peggy made him think of—sweetness and flowers with a touch of wild. But what she made him *feel* was even more incredible.

She opened her eyes then, slowly, as if she felt his eyes on her.

"Good morning," she said sleepily. Her green eyes were slightly hazy from sleep, her smile lovely and sensuous. She looked down at the brilliant bunch of flowers in her lap.

"An understatement," Mike said. His smile grew.

"Flowers?" she said. She lifted one up and breathed in the lovely fragrance. "Wildflowers are my favorites."

"I figured that." He sat beside her on the swing and began to rock it gently.

Peggy nudged him. "You don't think I'm the long-stemmed roses type, Kendrick? Is that what you're telling me?"

"I'm saying you're as beautiful as the flowers that grow natural and untouched in the field." He grinned and clasped his hands behind his head. "There, how's that?"

"A poet! I went to heaven with a poet." Peggy moved her legs and leaned comfortably into his side. She looked at his long tan legs, stretched out, glistening with tiny beads of perspiration. He was beautiful. Every bit of him, inside and out. This day, the night, surely it was a gift from some divine source. Surely. "Well?" she asked finally. She looked up at him through her tousled hair. "Tell me, Mr. Kendrick, do you still respect me?"

Mike paused for a long time. His brows lifted as he looked down his strong nose at her, his face a pretense of serious thought. Then he laughed loosely, a husky laugh that sent goose bumps down Peggy's arms.

"Don't laugh like that or look at me like that."

"Why not?" He dropped one hand onto her shoulder and began to massage it.

"Because it turns me to mush. It will keep me from eating whatever smells so wonderful in that white box. It will keep me from walking around the lake with you now, from catching the sunshine and..." The lump formed then and her words fell off.

Mike's hand slid down her shoulder, across the curve of her shoulder bone, down beneath the collar of the robe until his fingers were gently caressing her breast.

Peggy sighed and dropped her head back onto his shoulder.

"There's a time to eat and a time to walk, m'lady," he whispered into her hair. "But how about a shower first?"

FINALLY, AN HOUR LATER, they sat on the porch in jeans and T-shirts, devouring the sweet, buttery rolls and drinking cups of fresh coffee Peggy had brewed. She lifted a small crumb from the corner of Mike's mouth with the tip of her finger and set it on his tongue. It was an easy, familiar gesture, born of their lovemaking. She grinned. "I somehow have this urge to touch you."

"Urges should be satisfied, otherwise strange neuroses develop."

"That's what I've always thought," she said and they both laughed at the silliness, at the wonderful ease of being together.

"So, Mike, what's next?" Peggy said. She was licking the sweet cinnamon from her fingers in between words.

Mike found the small movement totally distracting. "What?" he said, frowning and pulling his eyes from her lips.

"What are we going to do today?"

Next. What was next? All he could see along the continuum of time was loving Peggy Shilling. He shook his head to clear his thoughts and then stood and took her hand, pulling her smoothly off the swing. "Next, my love, we go about the business of the day. And we better go soon, or it may be too late."

Peggy felt it, too, the wonderful pull inside her, the feeling that she and Mike, standing there separately, were necessary to each other. She felt complete, in a brand-new way. It was difficult not to touch him, not to wrap her arms around him, not to sink back onto the feathery quilt in the bedroom with him. Their eyes met then and they both laughed, light and lovely laughter that joined their souls. "Peggy, my dear, you're a witch," he said.

"You've cast a few spells yourself, Mike."

"I hope so," he said. "But spells or no spells, there are a few things I need to take care of."

"You do your business and I'll clean up here," she suggested. "And then—"

But Mike stopped her. "You'll do nothing of the kind," he said, wrapping an arm around her waist and pulling her toward the door. "I want you at my side every minute. And the business isn't the three-piece-suit kind. I need to deliver some papers to a fellow who works for us, that's all."

After a quick call to Carmen to check on Billy, they were on the road again, this time driving away from the inn and up into a hilly, forested area.

"Where are we going?"

"Up," Mike answered, then grinned at her and slipped in a tape. Peter Gabriel was singing about love.

After a while Mike pulled his car through a nonde-script gate and drove carefully up a winding, one-lane road that was hugged by stands of tall pine. "Here we are," he said a short while later, his voice bright with pleasure.

Peggy looked up. They were in a small clearing and in the distance was a clean, freshly painted building that looked like a barn. Behind it was a bright green meadow carved out of the woods. And to the right of the barn was a small house. It was toward the house that Mike headed as soon as they were out of the car. There was a lightness to his step, an excitement that Peggy found contagious, and she hurried alongside him.

"Sam? Anyone here?" Mike called out. They stepped up onto the porch of the small frame build-ing.

At that moment a short, barrel-chested man, gray-ing at the temples, opened the screen door. "Son of a gun! Didn't know you were coming today, Michael!"

He pumped the younger man's hand, then noticed Peggy. "Ah, and you've a lovely filly with you?"

Mike laughed. "This is Peggy Shilling. Peggy, meet Sam Hutchins. He runs this place."

Peggy smiled into the man's crinkly blue eyes. "Hi, Sam. Your place is beautiful!"

Sam laughed as if she had said something funny, and Mike explained, "This is the last vestige of the Kendrick land in these parts. The rest has all been turned into shopping centers and housing developments."

"They're good developments," Sam added. "But these acres left here, they're mighty special ones. We hope to hell Michael keeps them intact."

"Intact?" Peggy said. "This place is magnificent! Why wouldn't you?" She looked around at the stands of trees, the meadow, the incredible view down into the valley. They were on the very top of the hill, and off to one side she could see down to Paradise Lake.

Mike followed her gaze. "You recognize it? We've been winding our way through the woods around the lake. This land runs right down to the shore. Timber Lodge is directly across from here."

Peggy was in awe at the beauty. How anything this close to her home could have escaped her for all these years seemed almost cruel. This was so incredibly lovely, so clean and fresh. She looked at Sam, then Mike. "Why would this not be kept intact? I don't understand."

"Some big Chicago guns want to build a plant out here," Sam said. Then he looked at Mike. "They were out here sniffing around again last week. Said your old

man told them to spend as much time as they wanted.''
Peggy noticed that Sam's face was a mass of frowns as
he talked.

Mike laid a hand on Sam's shoulder. ''Don't worry,
Sam. My father knows how I feel about this land.''

''Hope to hell,'' Sam murmured.

Half-listening to the conversation, Peggy looked
down toward the lake again and wondered briefly if
the narrow strip of shoreline below was the place Mike
used to go with his father to fish.

She turned back toward Mike and Sam and asked
about the other buildings on the property.

''The wife and I live here,'' Sam said, nodding his
head toward the house behind him. ''That over
there—'' he pointed a short bent finger to the white
building Peggy had spotted as they drove in ''—that's
the stable. Then there's a few sheds for supplies. And
that's about it. The rest is three hundred acres of God-
made beauty. Nothing like it for miles around!''

''Sam's lived here forever. Takes good care of the
place.''

''I find hikers around and I let them have fun. What
the hell, I say, why not? Isn't that what the good Lord
intended with places like this?'' He didn't wait for an
answer. Instead he started walking toward the stable.
''Come on, Michael, bring your little lady along and
let's show off this place right.''

''Fine with me, Sam. Lead the way,'' Mike said.

He took Peggy's hand and they walked across the
clearing and down a slight incline to the large stable.
It was so natural, the way he took her hand, pulled her
close, brushed a strand of hair from her cheek. Peggy

smiled into the sunshine and squeezed the fingers that held her own.

When they reached the building Sam opened one of the double doors and ushered them inside.

Peggy looked around the cool darkness, her eyes adjusting to the dim light. Several stalls lined either side of the building, and in each one was a beautiful thoroughbred horse. "Oh, my," Peggy said, awed. She walked over to the first stall. "They're beautiful! Whose horses are they?"

"Mine and Sam's," Mike said.

"They're Michael's, missy. I'm the uncle."

Peggy wound her fingers gently in the auburn mane of a horse standing patiently in the first stall. Slowly she ran her fingers down the long, patrician nose and whispered soft words to the beast while Mike looked on in amazement.

"You know horses, Peg?"

"I knew one horse. My aunt Bessie—Maxie's mom—lived on a farm for a while. She had some horses and I spent some time out there. I loved that horse. He was my best friend."

She continued to pat the horse's nose, murmuring gently to it, and Mike continued to watch her, a whole mess of emotions collecting in his gut.

Finally Sam cleared his throat. "I think I'll leave you two for a bit. Work to be done, you know."

"Okay, Sam," Mike said. "There's some paperwork for the horse registrations in my briefcase."

"Right, boss," Sam said, then he tipped the Chicago Cubs hat topping his graying head and shuffled on out.

"Would you like to ride?" Mike asked. "I want to check some fencing and it's as good a way as any to get to it."

At that moment the stately mare beside Peggy dipped her elegant nose and nuzzled Peggy's neck. She laughed. "How can I say no to that? I'd love to."

Mike saddled two horses and led them out into the open air. He watched as Peggy gracefully swung her legs across the saddle, watched as she leaned forward and spoke to the horse. A rush of pleasure shot through him, unexplainable and powerful. Just the sight of her did it to him now, and somehow, seeing her with these beasts he'd raised from colts compounded it. He thought of Melanie and the one time he had brought her out to Sam's. She'd hated it. There were no proper bath facilities, the saddles weren't right and she didn't have her jodhpurs. It had been a disaster, and both he and Melanie had felt bad about it later. But here was Peggy, acting as if she'd been born on Lady, whispering horse talk into the animal's ear. He brought his horse up beside her, leaned over, and before she knew he was there, he kissed her.

She giggled. "What was that for?"

"Happiness," he said simply.

And then they left the meadow and Mike pointed toward the woods and a rutted trail that entered it on the west. He let Peggy take the lead and brought his horse up a few gaits behind her. She sat the thoroughbred with beautiful calm, her slender back straight and her shoulders and arms perfectly relaxed. With a careless, confident toss of her head, she threw him a breathtaking smile and took off.

He let out a slow breath, his eyes shining. *I'll be damned,* he thought, and he spurred his mount into a fast trot to catch up with her as she disappeared into the woods.

The pathway wound through the woods, around the area of fencing Mike needed to check, and then sloped gradually down to the shore of the lake. They stopped and dismounted when they reached the water, stretching their legs and offering the horses a cool drink. Peggy's hair was tangled from the breeze and her face glowed from the exercise. She slid down on the sandy beach beside Mike and put her hand on his bent knee.

"This is wonderful, Mike. I could get used to all this very quickly—the ride, you, the country...."

Mike threaded his fingers through the tangle of her hair. "Well, darlin', we'll have to see what we can do about that. You were born to the saddle, that's plain."

Peggy laughed. She leaned slightly against him and welcomed the river of pleasure the nearness brought to her. "Funny how we two city slickers fit in here," she drawled.

"Like ducks in water," he said.

"Eskimos in igloos."

"Cherries in pie."

"Stars in the sky."

"A kiss on lips." Slowly, surely, Mike lowered her back on the soft, hot sand and kissed her.

"Now you're talking," Peggy murmured. She wrapped her arms around his neck and held him tight. She didn't want to ever let go, not of Mike, nor the day, nor the incredible happiness that filled her so completely she thought she might burst.

He kissed her again, and then again, and each time Peggy returned his kiss with all the lovely emotion spiraling around inside her.

It was much later when they returned to the stable and handed the horses over to Sam to be cooled down and brushed. Mike introduced Peggy to Sam's wife, Ella, a tiny woman with crinkly eyes and a hearty laugh who served them a late but enormous lunch, and then they were off again, driving back to the inn to collect their bags.

"I don't want to leave, Mike," Peggy said. "Not ever. This is a wonderful, special place."

Mike nodded thoughtfully. "I've thought for a while now of building a place up here," he said. "There's a perfect spot up on the land near the stable that overlooks the lake."

"Right above where you used to fish with your father?"

He looked at her with surprise, then laughed. "Yes. That's right where I had in mind. Only now I remember that spot for other reasons."

"Why haven't you? Built a place, I mean."

Mike shrugged. "I don't know. The idea comes to me, and then life gets in the way. You know how it is. I wouldn't live here all the time, but everyone needs a hobby, and I guess this is mine—the horses, the land. Being out here, riding through the woods, puts all the other business into perspective, and I feel more able to handle all the deals and company problems after a dose of this."

"Well, I say go for it. You're different up here, Mike."

"If I'm different this weekend, darlin', I don't think it has much to do with the land."

The look he gave her sent her heart spinning crazily and she lowered her head to hide the flush that covered her cheeks.

He tipped up her chin. "Know what I mean?"

This time she kept her eyes steady, locked into his. "Yes, Mike," she said slowly. "I know exactly what you mean."

"Well, anyway—" He ran a finger along her cheek, down over her lips, and looked at her for a long time. He felt the knot in his throat, the longing, the tightness in his chest.

Peggy watched him curiously. Watched the emotion flit across his face, glaze his eyes. What an incredible dance this all was, she thought. And where would they each be when the music stopped, when the dance ended? Would they be together . . . or at the opposite ends of the earth?

And for one brief moment she felt a flicker of fear, a threat to this happiness that she was determined to hang on to for at least a little while.

She forced a bright smile to her face, lifted up on her toes and kissed Mike lightly. "Come on, cowboy, we'd better get going."

The drive back was quiet. Peggy found herself reaching over to touch Mike, on his cheek, the side of his head, his arm. "You're driving me crazy, Peggy," he growled. He wound her fingers tightly in his own and held her hand on his thigh, kept it there as an anchor for the rest of the ride home. Linked together they could ward off the world that would impose itself on them only too soon.

When they finally reached her apartment Peggy sat there for a minute in quiet, not moving to leave. Mike, too, was reluctant to break the spell, to end the day.

Finally Peggy leaned over and brushed a kiss across his lips.

"Has there ever, in the history of the whole universe, been a day this beautiful?"

"No," Mike answered. "There never has, but we'll see to it, my love, that it isn't the last."

Chapter Ten

Peggy and Mike had invented romance. Peggy was absolutely certain of it.

Her life took on a heady pace. Daily jobs, routines, were propelled by a passion that left her feeling exuberant, intoxicated, and she yearned for the moments when she and Mike could be together.

One night she cooked for Mike in her apartment, a chance for him, she said, to be cooled by her Kendrick-sponsored air conditioner. She had run over to Otto's Market after work, her heart giddy with anticipation at seeing Mike.

The deli shop was empty when she arrived.

"Otto!" she called out.

The butcher appeared instantly from the back room, his white brows pulled together.

"What is this? A fire? What's all this screaming? Ack, it's you, Peggy. What's the matter, dear heart?" He wiped his hands on his white apron.

"Matter? Nothing's the matter, Otto. Everything's right. Everything's astonishingly, wonderfully right."

"I can see that, Peggy. Yes, I can."

He squinted his eyes and looked at Peggy for a long time, then broke out into a broad grin and lifted a thin, bent finger into the air. "Aha!" he said. "Now I understand. It's a man."

Peggy's eyes crinkled with laughter. "A man? No, Otto...it's *the* man, the most wonderful man in the world."

Otto grinned. "My little scamp is in love!"

Peggy's eyes widened. Although Carmen had said the same thing to her, Peggy had refused to acknowledge it out loud. She *did* love Mike, loved him in an incredible, euphoric, all-encompassing way. But it was her secret, held tightly in her heart, and she was going to have to come up with a way to stop it from pouring out in front of everyone from the mailman to her butcher.

Acknowledged love meant planning, talk of futures, lives together, and she and Mike weren't ready for that yet. No, best to enjoy all this now, to leave the future alone for a bit.

She tilted her chin up and looked Otto in the eye. "Love? Otto, what a thing to say! A nice girl like me? Come on, now, help me with this dinner—please?"

Otto laughed his deep, gravelly laugh and said, "Okeydokey. Sure enough, little one, you can stop that blushing business, we'll talk food. Okay, we'll make it perfect. Perfecto! Now, what is he like, then we'll know what to fix."

"What he is like? Hmm." Peggy leaned one elbow up on the counter. "He is like fresh snow. He is a mountain man, a kind gentle strong funny handsome man. He is a city man, a Renaissance man, a...a..."

"No, no! What is he *like*, little one? Does he like music? Or skiing? Or swimming in the ocean? Does he like vegetables? Fish? Fresh game? Does he like movies? Opera? Books? *That* will tell us what to fix."

Peggy lifted her brows uncertainly.

Otto grinned. "Okay, okay, don't worry. He is a wonderful man. I know what to fix. He will love this." And he dished up a bountiful supply of his chicken cacciatore—all prepared and ready to eat. Then he added fresh rolls, a bottle of wine and strawberry cheesecake to the package. "Now *this* is what you feed him, Peggy."

"But I was going to *cook* dinner, Otto—"

"Shh," the old man said, wagging his finger in the air. "Tonight *I* cook, and you sit with your young man and find out if he likes books or opera or square dancing or the two-step. Tonight you do that—next time you cook."

And that is exactly what she did. She set the table and lit the candles and served up Otto's mouthwatering meal. Mike ate with relish, as if he'd never tasted anything so fine, and while Billy slept soundly they peeled away new layers of one another.

"I played the tuba in seventh grade," Peggy confessed.

"Trumpet," Mike said, his mouth half-full. He pushed his empty plate aside and reached for the remains of Peggy's.

"Country western swept me up when I was fourteen—"

Mike groaned. "Noooo!"

"For two weeks," she said quickly.

And they discovered that they both loved Vivaldi and Mozart, Peter Gabriel and Simon and Garfunkel, disliked Andy Warhol paintings, loved the Impressionists, some contemporary art and supported the women's movement. Mike didn't hunt, and Peggy was silently relieved. He was a strong swimmer and skier, a fair golfer, had never played soccer, and challenged Peggy to a tennis match the next week.

"You're looking at all-city, Mike," Peggy warned him with a menacing grin, and he responded by wrapping her in his arms and kissing away her frowns and threats. Mike loved every kind of food he could think of except beets. Peggy tossed hominy in the never-touch heap, and they both grinned. "Yeah, hominy leaves me cold," Mike agreed.

And when they were all through, after the last small crumb of Otto's cheesecake was gone and Mike had driven away into the black night, the ties were strengthened, and it didn't have much to do with likes or dislikes. Mike made Peggy feel whole and in touch with life in a way she had never been before. Otto was right. Peggy was in love.

A FEW NIGHTS LATER they had agreed to tend to family affairs, Peggy to cook dinner for her cousin Maxie, and Mike to dine and spend time with his parents, a task that he'd neglected lately.

"Michael," his mother said as she ushered him into the library, "this is far too long to stay away, darling."

"I've been busy, mother," he answered noncommittally.

"No more than usual, your father tells me. Sit down and fill me in on what is going on in your life."

Mike smiled. He knew his mother's interest was sincere, but he also knew that if he waited long enough he wouldn't have to say a word; she would take over the conversation.

Claire nodded to the butler to bring them cocktails. Then she lifted her glasses from a tapestry case and put them on. "But before your father comes in, Michael, and while I have you all to myself, we need to formalize some dates." Claire Kendrick opened an elaborate gilt-edged appointment book on the desk and carefully turned the slick pages. After reciting a few unimportant events that didn't involve Michael, she turned to the next week's dates. "Aha, here it is. You do know that we will all be together next week at the charity ball for Children's Hospital." She removed her glasses and looked up at Michael, waiting for his acknowledgment.

"Charity ball?" Mike frowned. For an instant he didn't know anything about balls or engagements or social responsibilities. Somehow it had all left when Peggy walked into his life. Priorities had shifted.

"The ball, Michael. Of course you remember. Melanie has been doing wonderful, exhausting work preparing for it. Your father and I have purchased a table for all of us—your sisters, you and Melanie, Joseph and Nancy. Grams. There will be eleven of us. I don't like to have an odd number but Grandmother Kendrick insists she feels up to going."

Michael was about to volunteer his absence to make the numbers more convenient, but he stopped himself in time to avoid his mother's displeasure. He remembered now—Melanie and Nancy's committee work, the gala charity event. He had promised Melanie that he'd escort her, so of course he'd go—but the thought of it was nearly foreign to him. It was a part of another existence, not the one that had occupied him these past weeks with Peggy.

"Your tuxedo is clean, of course?"

Mike was relieved when his father came in and the conversation took its usual turn from social to business topics. R.J. had several people with him, business associates who would be staying for dinner, and that, too, pleased Michael. He didn't want his mother to have a chance to pry into his life; above all, he didn't want to talk with her about Peggy.

During the main course Mike received his first surprise of the evening.

"That land up in Wisconsin is great land," R.J. was saying over the beef tenderloin. "Picturesque, easy to get to, no zoning problems."

Michael frowned. "You sound like a salesman."

R.J. laughed. "Son, when you're selling something, that's what you sound like."

"You're not selling the Wisconsin land?"

R.J. looked at the man sitting across from him, then back to his son. "I haven't had a chance to talk with you yet, Michael, but you know as well as I do that we have enough developments up there. Clarence is interested in the land as an annex for his plant. Perfect place, up in those hills. Give the farmers some business. The unemployed in the area would have jobs.

Labor's plentiful. It sounds like a good idea to me. We'll have to see.''

Mike looked at his father. The conversation had already moved along to other things and his father was laughing at something a guest had said. Claire was motioning to the servants to clear the table, and Mike was fuming. Sell the land? Over his dead body would his father sell that land.

The second surprise came later, over coffee on the patio. The night had cooled and after the guests left, Mike joined his mother and father outside for a few minutes before leaving himself.

"Dad, it's late and now's not the right time to talk about it, but promise me one thing—that you won't reach a decision on the land until we've talked." Mike was standing near his father, his hands shoved in the pockets of his suit pants.

"Of course, my boy. That's understood."

"Good."

"Now sit down for two minutes and have a cigar. Cuban. Damn good."

Mike didn't like cigars, but it seemed to mellow his father to be joined in his after-dinner smoke, so he sat down and took the offered cigar, the glass of iced coffee, the splash of brandy. He stretched his legs, loosened his tie and looked off into the black night, his thoughts turning to Peggy.

As if he knew, his father asked, "How is the young woman working out—that Peg girl?"

"Peggy is working out fine. The project is almost finished, but Joe is thinking he'd like to keep her on

to help with some other things. He says she has a real
aptitude for the work.''

R.J. nodded, his face expressionless. Finally he said,
''She's spunky.''

Mike smiled. ''I guess you could say that. She's a lot
of things.''

''Do you see her?'' his mother asked then, her
brows lifting carefully.

''You mean outside of work, I suppose.''

''Yes.''

''Yes. I'd have brought her along tonight but she
was busy. In fact, she's spending the evening with her
cousin Maxie, your maid.''

''Oh, Maxine,'' Claire said.

Mike nodded.

''Actually,'' Claire said slowly, ''she isn't our maid
any longer.''

''She quit?''

''No, I terminated her employment.''

''Why?''

''It wasn't working out.''

Mike frowned. ''She wasn't good at it?''

''Oh, she was all right, but it seemed awkward, and
I thought I would spare your friend Peggy embarrassment, should you ever bring her back for dinner.''

''What?'' Mike stood and looked down at his
mother. She'd fired Maxie! ''Mother, I can't believe
you did that. Peggy wasn't embarrassed that her
cousin worked here—it's an honest job, she wasn't
running drugs or selling her body. And the kid needed
the job. She's working her way through school!''

"Michael, keep your voice down when you speak to your mother."

It was R.J.'s contribution, the arbitrator, keeping the rules of decorum intact. It fueled Mike's anger. He loved his parents, but God knows he would never understand them! "Why, mother, why did you fire her?" he asked now.

"Michael, I have a great deal more experience in matters like this than you do. You'll simply have to trust my judgment here. It was the appropriate thing to do. And I didn't leave the young woman destitute, for heaven's sake. We gave her two months' severance pay, which is certainly more than generous."

After leaving his parents, Mike found himself driving aimlessly for a while along the lake. He couldn't shake the anger over Maxie's firing. As the cool lake breeze calmed him, he thought back over the years and realized there had been hundreds of firings and hirings that had gone on under his nose, many, probably, for even less provocation. But he had never noticed, never cared. And, he had to admit, he wouldn't have noticed this time if Max hadn't been Peggy's cousin. He wondered briefly if *he* had done any of that at Kendrick Enterprises, any needless disrupting of people's lives for less than credible reasons. Probably, he thought sadly. He probably had.

PEGGY SHOWED UP the next day at Mike's office door, a white sack in hand, and told him she was treating him to lunch. "Leftovers," she said. "Otto talked me into enough lasagna to feed an army last night, and for old times' sake I thought I'd share it with you."

"Cold lasagna?" Mike said skeptically.

"Don't knock it until you've tried it."

They ate it off paper plates in the park across from Mike's office, and it wasn't until they were finished that Mike asked about her evening with Maxie.

"We had a wonderful time, so much to catch up on. Maxie is wonderful. She's majoring in chemical engineering—I barely know what that *means*—and I know someday she'll do great things."

"Peg—"

Peggy stood abruptly, crumpled up the lunch sack and threw it into a trash can. "I know. Maxie told me she wasn't working for your parents anymore."

There was a set to Peggy's jaw as she spoke.

Mike sighed.

"Max wasn't complaining," Peggy went on. "In fact, she wouldn't have mentioned it at all, I don't think, but I asked her about it, joking, wondering if she'd dropped pie on anyone recently."

"My mother is old-fashioned, Peg."

Peggy looked at him. Her eyes were dark and looked up from under the wave of auburn fringe that swept across her forehead. "I don't know what your mother is, Mike. Maxie said she was gracious. She offered to help her find another job, but Maxie wouldn't let her. The reason she gave Maxie was vague and of course not the real one, which was me, my being there."

Mike's eyes darkened. "It's complicated, Peggy. Does she need a job? I'll give her a job, Peg."

Peggy shook her head. "Mike, everything is so easily fixed for you. I mean, you replace things so easily.

But life doesn't work like that. Can you understand that people might not want you to fix everything for them?'' Before he could answer she went on, ''No, you probably can't. You're kind and good, Mike, but you see things from here—'' Her hand shot up in the air. ''And I see things from here, from the park bench or the subway. Different planets.''

She shook her head and looked at him, her eyes as large as Mike had ever seen them. The look in them was so sad that it squeezed the breath out of him and Mike could barely answer her. She looked grieved, and it nearly tore him apart. He wrapped his arms around her, held her to his chest and breathed in the fresh scent of her hair. ''Peggy, Peggy,'' he said, ''oh, how I love you.''

THAT NIGHT PEGGY TURNED the words over and over in her mind. *Peggy, I love you.* It was the first time Mike had spoken them, but once was enough. She would hug them to her heart and never forget them. He loved her. She loved him. Ammunition, certainly, to get them over small things like hirings and firings. She resolved then and there to lighten up, to fling herself entirely into this wonderful new chapter in her life.

BUT IT WAS ENERVATING. Between being a mother, planning for Casey's wedding, working extra hours with the clown troupe and being in love, Peggy was exhausted, and sometimes her resolve weakened and the trickle of fear ran stronger.

She sank into a chair at Casey's lake-view condo a few days later and sighed. "Casey, life is moving too fast for me."

Casey handed her a cold beer. "That, my dear, dear friend, is because you are in love, and there simply aren't enough hours in the day to handle it."

"It's so confusing."

"Only if you let it, Pegs. Look at Pete and me—I love him to death, and it's not confusing at all."

"But you and Pete moved into it naturally, gradually. *Normally.*"

Casey frowned. "I don't know if I should pursue that line of thinking or not. Now guzzle that beer and help me plan this wedding."

Billy was sitting in the corner of the room, pounding on an assortment of pots and pans Casey had taken out of the cupboard. Casey looked over at him. "Shall I have Billy play at the ceremony or just the reception?"

Peggy laughed. "Case, sometimes I can't believe you're getting married." And then suddenly, without any warning, the tears began to fall.

"Peggy, are you all right? What's wrong, hon? Hey, I *love* Pete. This is a *good* thing."

Peggy nodded and reached for a tissue.

Casey walked over and wrapped an arm around Peggy's shoulders. "Peggy, you're an emotional mess. Listen, Mike Kendrick is a good man. A wonderful man. And he loves you like crazy. I can see it in his eyes, in the way he talks to you, looks at you. And you, *you*, I've never seen you more alive, more beautiful. Now throw the worries away, hon, and go with it. Enjoy what you have. And who knows, soon I may be helping *you* plan a wedding.''

Sometimes Peggy caught herself thinking that way, in terms of weddings and planning for the future. But just as quickly as the thoughts came she pushed them aside. For now she wanted to simply relish the present, not complicate it with anything but what it was.

Chapter Eleven

"How do I look?" Peggy did a fake curtsy and her brilliant red hair flew in hundreds of directions at once. She tapped one gigantic saddle shoe against the floor.

Maxie had come along to help her dress and she looked at her cousin now, carefully scrutinizing her from head to toe. "I've never seen you look better, Peggy," she said. She patted Peggy's flyaway hair back into place. "A little more rouge, maybe."

Peggy bent down and looked into the mirror, then frowned. "More, you think? Well, okay." She took the fat makeup stick and rubbed it into her cheeks, brightening the circle of color. "There." She stood back and stuck her thumbs behind the thick suspenders that held up her baggy silk pants. A bright pink blouse with full sleeves and a plaid bow tie completed her outfit. "Perfect," Max said. "I like the new pants. They're you."

"Think so?" Peggy picked up a tiny bowl-like black hat with a lone daisy sticking out of the rim and pushed it into the bed of red hair.

"Definitely," said Maxie. "If Mike Kendrick could only see you now!"

Max's final comment set both her and Peggy laughing. Peggy twirled her folded plaid umbrella around and began to sing. "If he could see me now…"

And then she sobered a little. She had been too busy, and Mike, as well, to squeeze in much time together this week. And not seeing him affected her whole being. When they could catch each other they connected over the phone, but it wasn't the same as touching him, loving him. Hopefully once tonight was behind her, and with Joe's project nearing an end, they'd have more time together.

"Time to go, Dr. Laugh A. Lot," Maxie said, and Peggy pulled herself from her thoughts, gave Maxie her best clown smile and grabbed her stethoscope.

Max held open the door and together they walked down the long hall and toward the elegant ballroom that was to hold tonight's extraordinary gala, the circus beneath the stars.

Every dollar made from tonight's party would go to the Children's Hospital, and Peggy and the others in the clown troupe—the whole company who worked tirelessly with the ill children every week—had been invited as part of the program. Some of the money raised from tonight's ball was earmarked for the troupe and the board thought it would be good for the benefactors to experience the clowns firsthand. They were to circulate throughout the ballroom in their costumes, play their musical instruments, blow their fanciful bubbles, juggle and display all the other wonderful talents that brought laughter and love and hope to the children. Peggy had laughed when another hospital clown had described their function at tonight's ball as living decorations, the newest thing in society hype. Oh, well, she'd concentrate on the new children's wing that would become a reality because of events like this. And in between, if there were any quiet moments when she could escape into the shadows, she'd concentrate on Mike. And *those* thoughts could get her through anything.

THE BALL WAS BEING HELD in one of Chicago's largest and finest hotels. The ballroom was a breathtaking, elegant fairyland, the result of hundreds of hours of work by Chicago's most dedicated socialites.

The Kendricks arrived en masse and walked together into the hotel. Claire Kendrick, looking elegant in a black Armani evening dress, was the first to enter the ballroom. She stopped on the wide carpeted steps and looked around, taking in everything—the round dinner tables covered with pink and green and daffodil yellow linens, the colored trapeze swings that hung from the high ceilings and held life-size dolls swinging slowly back and forth. Silver balloons were collected in elegant bouquets and on the tables brightly painted circus animals held napkins, silver baskets were filled with fresh yellow and pink roses, gilt-edged plates and crystal glasses sparkled in candlelight. Waiters dressed as ringmasters and performers circulated among the guests, offering Bellinis and wine and caviar. And over to one side a magnificent calliope, its brass pipes shining in the glow of the candles and crystal chandeliers, lured the partygoers to the circus ball with its distinctive whistlelike music.

"Melanie, my dear," Claire said, "this is extraordinary." She reached for Melanie's hand.

"Thank you, but Nancy and I only did the tables, Claire," she said modestly, but her protestations did nothing to diminish Claire Kendrick's high praise.

A hostess in a long, form-fitting sequined gown with a tiny balloon corsage indicating her position then led the entire party, including Grams, looking alert and elegant in a breathtaking Balenciaga gown she had owned for forty years, to their table. Mike trailed the others and looked around at the festive decorations as he wove his way between the tables. But his mind was elsewhere. He had tried to reach Peggy just before leaving his parents' home where they had all met for precocktail cocktails. He needed to hear her voice, to somehow touch her, even if over the wires of the phone. The week had been hectic, and he felt an uncomfortable empty spot in the very center of him because he hadn't held her now for two days.

"You're a lost cause, Kendrick," Joe had told him that morning. "But I approve. Peggy's quite a woman." Joe had paused then, looking down at some papers on the desk, struggling with a decision. Finally he'd looked up at Mike.

Mike had been watching him curiously. "Hey, Joe, if you have something to say, say it."

"No offense?"

"When has that ever bothered you, Paling?" Mike had teased. "Come on, out with it."

"I like Peggy a lot, Michael. She's solid. But she has some strengths that might make it difficult for her to merge easily into—"

"Yeah, I know," Mike had said, his words overlapping Joe's. Mike had looked out the window, then back to Joe. "Did you know my mother fired her cousin because she thought it awkward for a guest to be related to the help?"

"That's exactly the kind of thing I mean."

"My family doesn't rule my life, Joe."

"I know that, too. It might be more than your family, though. Some things you can't shake, Mike. Some things are with you from birth. It's a whole life—"

"You live the same kind of life as I do."

"But it's different for me. I wasn't born to it, Mike. I'm not *of* that life—I'm simply rich." He'd laughed then and the mood had been lightened.

"I know what you're saying, Joe," Mike had said. "You're a good friend, and I appreciate it. But if there is one person on earth I'd slay dragons to prevent from hurting, it's Peggy."

"Okay. Well, good," Joe had replied. He'd grabbed an athletic bag from the floor and nodded toward the door. "Now come on, Kendrick, and let me whip your tail at racquetball. I'll show you birthright isn't everything it's cracked up to be."

MIKE THOUGHT BACK OVER the conversation now as he was seated at the elegant table, and he hypothesized about bringing Peggy to this ball. She could have fit in because she was bright and beautiful and could have *made* herself fit in, but she wouldn't have liked it. No, she wouldn't have liked it at all. That brought a smile to his eyes, and spotting it across the table Joe lifted his glass to Mike in a silent toast.

Dinner was served by fire-eaters and trapeze artists and lion tamers; flaming desserts were carried in by sword throwers. It was an elegant extravaganza. At the end of dinner, before the dancing began, introductions of hospital VIPs and ball organizers were made. Melanie and Nancy and other committee heads were acknowledged and encouraged to stand and be applauded for their tireless efforts. And then the hospital CEO thanked everyone for all the work and explained a little bit about the special people who would be circulating the rest of the evening, the marvelous troupe of clowns who devoted hours to the patients at Children's Hospital.

As the orchestra played "Here Come the Clowns," they came out onto the dance floor en masse, Dr. E. Z. Duzzit, Dr. Windowpain, Dr. T.L.C., Dr. Laugh A. Lot and the rest. They were blowing square bubbles, playing tunes on stethoscopes, juggling pill vials and sneezing rainbows of colored streamers.

The hundreds of elegantly dressed women and handsome, tuxedoed men applauded them warmly. Then the orchestra switched to other pieces and couples glided over to the dance floor while the clowns "worked the crowd," as Peggy had described it earlier to Maxie.

"Aren't they cute?" Nancy said to Joe.

"They do good things with the children, I hear," Claire Kendrick said. "Occasionally, however, it's been rather raucous when I've been volunteering. I think they need to calm them down some. The children are very sick, after all.''

"I'm sure the doctors would stop it if there was a problem," Mike said. "Even sick kids need to have fun." He thought of the possibility of Billy being sick, of how grateful he'd be to any clown who could make him smile.

A pair of clowns stopped at their table then, and the conversation dropped off while one clown played "Star Dust" on bagpipes made from inflated rubber gloves and the other accompanied him with a flute made out of a syringe.

Thoroughly enjoying the added attraction, Mike and Joe encouraged the clowns and they obliged, lingering at the Kendrick table, flirting, and performing a funny-bone transplant on R.J. himself. Mike's thoughts turned again to Peggy. She'd love this. She worked with clowns herself, although he wasn't exactly sure what she did. But this group was terrific and he'd have to remember the details so he could describe it all to her tomorrow.

But thoughts of Peggy persisted, and finally, unnoticed by the rest of the table who were still intrigued with the clowns, he slipped away in search of a phone. Grams had always insisted that if a person remained in one's thoughts for a long time there was probably a reason, and the best policy was to get in touch with that person. So he would, just to hear her voice, to say good-night.

Across the room Peggy soon discovered that she had quite a flair for performing, and the time went by quickly. People were gracious, enjoying the clown antics and asking intelligent questions about the clowns' work at the hospital. It was proving to be a wonderful way to spread PR without cramming it down people's throats.

Peggy and Dr. T.L.C. had nearly circled the room, were almost ready to call it a night, when the floor fell out from beneath her.

She stared at the table. R.J. and Mrs. Kendrick, Joe, Grams and those two elegant women—Melanie and Nancy something—who had each in turn made her feel she needed an appointment at Elizabeth Arden ASAP. But no Mike. At least that was a relief, although the empty seat next to Melanie was very suspicious. She had been thinking of Mike all night, but this wasn't where she wanted him to materialize, not with his whole family sitting there and with her dressed as a clown. They looked so complete, so beautiful, so picture perfect. The *ideal* family, she thought.

And then her heart began to beat erratically, and she chastised herself furiously for not preparing for this. Where was her head? How could she have been so stupid? Of *course* the Kendricks would be here—it was the social event of the season! But Mike hadn't mentioned it . . .

Stacia—Dr. T.L.C.—had already gotten the attention of the Kendrick table and was standing several feet away in a small open space. Peggy's options were to disappear quietly into the crowd and leave her partner embarrassed and alone, or to continue on as if nothing were different. She took a deep breath and joined Stacia.

Peggy looked around the table. Although they had certainly seen her, most of them, except for Grams, were watching Stacia juggle nurse's caps, and she hadn't seen any flickers of recognition. Peggy swallowed hard and kept her smile in place. They might not recognize her at all. Except for Joe, they had met her only once or twice, and she had enough theater makeup on tonight that she had barely recognized herself.

With that thought bolstering up her shaky legs, she picked up her stethoscope and with special clown magic she began blowing beautiful square bubbles out of its end.

MIKE WENT TO THE BAR in the lobby and picked up a drink, then slowly walked back toward the ballroom. Peggy hadn't been home when he'd called. Carmen had offered some sort of explanation but she was whispering so low because of a sleeping Billy in her lap that Mike couldn't make out what she was saying. Maybe she was with Casey, he thought. She was excited about her friend's wedding, he knew, and involved in some of the preparations. That was probably it.

He felt a twinge at not telling Peggy he was coming to this thing tonight. She never pushed him for explanations, in fact she was just the opposite, but he should have told her, anyway. The plain truth was he'd forgotten about the damn thing. It wasn't important to him, and in the past few weeks he'd tended to put things like charity balls as far out of his mind as possible. It was, he told Joe one day, the "Peggy effect." Changed his attitude toward a whole slew of things.

He nursed his drink until it was gone, then set it on an empty table and walked slowly back toward his table.

Peggy first saw him out of the corner of her eye, a tall, exceedingly handsome man in a black tuxedo. And then he came more clearly into focus and her heart lurched to a stop.

She continued to blow her bubbles, bigger and bigger bubbles that distorted her face and filled the air around her. Stacia opened a large box and proceeded to capture Peggy's bubbles, slipping them into the box and holding them there by placing a lid on it. Then, with a grin and a flourish, Stacia opened the box and instead of bubbles she pulled out a bell and handed it to Peggy, and then another bell until they each had several, and while their audience sat in rapt attention they proceeded to play "Good night Ladies" on their colored bells, smiling and doing a little two-step that Peggy had thought so clever a few days ago when they had done it for the kids on Ward C. Tonight she felt ridiculous. But this was it, their finale, and then they could escape into the crowd of strangers.

It was Gram's eyes Peggy inadvertently caught as the last stanza of the song was rung on the bells. Grams, whose eyesight was nearly gone, whose face lit up in recognition and whose mouth began to move. But it was Mike's voice that broke into the ringing of the bells and called out, "Oh, my God, it's Peggy!" for the whole wide world to hear.

If only she had known this was going to happen, she thought vaguely, she wouldn't have needed rouge. Her face must be at least as scarlet as Nancy's stunning off-the-shoulder dress. She mustered a smile, looked at Mike directly and said brightly, "Hi, everybody."

Joe was laughing, an enthusiastic, glad-to-see-you kind of laugh. And Mike seemed truly happy. That helped somewhat. But the less-than-happy surprise on Mrs. Kendrick's face and the shaded disapproval on R.J.'s made Peggy want to disappear into the basket of flowers.

"I didn't know, Peg—you didn't tell me you were going to be here. I had no idea—" By that time Mike was around the table, his arm about her shoulders, his eyes taking in her costume and makeup and the embarrassment that coated her forehead and neck. "You look wonderful, Dr. Laugh A. Lot," he said simply. "Absolutely wonderful." He introduced Peggy to the couple of people at the table she hadn't met, his younger sister and his two brothers-in-law. "And I think everyone else here has met Peggy, right?" he asked.

Peggy watched as heads nodded silently, as eyes looked at her curiously.

"Peggy, dear, you are magnificent!" It was Grams, and Peggy went over and hugged her thin shoulders.

"It *is* wonderful, Grams," she said quietly. Her head was beginning to clear, her heartbeat to slow. "I love doing this. Not like this, not here, but for the kids. It's a good thing."

"Some day, my dear, I want to come with you to the hospital. I want to see the real thing. Will you do that?"

Peggy nodded and smiled at her gratefully. Then at Joe, whose wink and grin made her know the world hadn't completely collapsed.

"Can you join us, Peg?" Mike asked. "I can get another chair—"

"I'm sure Peggy has duties," Claire said, her tone gracious but firm.

"Yes!" Peggy said quickly. "I mean, no, not here. We're finished here, but I need to get home. Billy, you know..." She spoke to Mrs. Kendrick but her eyes sought Mike's.

He touched her arm. "Sure, of course, Peggy." He saw her discomfort and could have kicked himself. She was being put on display in front of all these people. All he had thought of at first was how glad he was to see her. But here she was, in the middle of his staid family, dressed as a clown. He wanted to pick her up, to carry her off, to protect her, love her. Instead he looked into her eyes and into her soul and said, "I have a new appreciation for clowns, Dr. Laugh A. Lot. Thank you."

Peggy half smiled, wanted to kiss him, to hold him to her and hear him tell her it was okay, but instead she tore her eyes away, said her goodbyes around the table as quickly as decorum allowed, and fled across the room.

Grams looked up as she fled. "Now there is a woman," she said, and then looked at Michael. "I do believe it's about time we showed the folks here a thing or two about dancing, don't you think, Michael?"

Chapter Twelve

Peggy's dreams that night were troubled, filled with images of sinister clowns dressed in elegant dresses, long hallways without light at the end, rooms without doors.

She awoke with a start. Sun was shining in the window, noises filtered in from the street and Billy was calling for a bottle. Peggy shook herself free of the disturbing sensations, brushed aside the remnants of sleep and began her day.

She tried not to think back to the night before, to the encounter with the Kendricks and to the feeling that followed her home and disturbed her sleep. Mike had been wonderful. But even the love she saw in his eyes, the kindness in his voice, couldn't rid her of the heaviness with which the evening left her.

Maxie had spent the night at Peggy's, and she thought the whole evening had been incredible and that the surprise encounter with the Kendricks a kick. "The clowns were the highlight, Peggy," she said. "All the stuffiness seemed to go out of people when they saw you."

"Sure, Maxie," Peggy said, and quickly swallowed a swig of strong black coffee.

The rest of the day went by in a blur. She spent it helping Casey finalize wedding plans and thinking of Mike. Missing Mike. And then chiding herself for missing someone she had seen a brief twelve hours before. But seeing him at the ball hadn't been seeing him the way she was used to. It had been worse than not seeing him at all.

"Yes, that's it!" she blurted out to Casey as they tossed caterers' menus back and forth between them.

"That's what, Pegs? What are you talking about?"

"That's the problem. The problem is seeing him with his family as a backdrop. They're everything I'm not, Case."

Casey didn't need to have the pronouns explained. "Pegs, you're twenty-seven years old. Michael Kendrick is, what? Thirty-five?"

"Four."

"You're not children. I mean, you and I have *no* immediate family, Pete has a normal family, Michael Kendrick happens to have an abnormal family. What difference does any of it make? Relationships involve two people, not the whole damn family tree, for heaven's sake!"

Peggy reached over on the couch and hugged her. "That's why you're my best friend, because you say things like that." Then she sat back and the smile fell away. "But it's more than that, Casey. When I say they're everything I'm not, it isn't that I'm sad about that. I don't *want* to be what they are. There isn't any way on earth I could live with all the baggage they carry, and I don't just mean *things,* I mean..." She paused for the right words and Casey spoke up.

"I think I know what you mean, Peggy, but what I said still holds. Mike is too terrific a guy to try to force you into the mold in which the Kendrick dynasty is shaped. No way he'd do that. I think what he loves about you is everything *they*'re not."

Peggy nibbled on her bottom lip. "Maybe." She wished he had called, wished she had talked to him after the ball, wished he'd take the fog out of her head. "You know, Case, we haven't talked about the future at all. He hasn't mentioned what's going to happen to us."

"Why should you wait for *him* to mention it, Pegs? You're a full half of this relationship, you know."

Peggy nodded thoughtfully and began flipping through a new menu. Why hadn't she brought it up? Why hadn't *he?* Were they both so frightened of the emotion they'd given birth to that they didn't want to shake its fragile being with talk of the future?

It was nearly dark when Peggy got home. Billy was almost asleep as she paid the cabdriver and carried her son clumsily up the steps. Billy's bulk prevented her from seeing the figure sitting quietly on the steps, and it wasn't until she tried to get her key into the lock that he spoke.

"Where've you been?" he asked, unbending his cramped legs and rising up beside her. "I haven't been able to reach you all day."

"Mike!" Billy lurched at the noise and then put his head back on Peggy's shoulder and closed his eyes again.

"Mike," she said more softly, "what are you doing here?"

Mike took the key from her hand and unlocked the door, ushered her through and then carefully took Billy from her arms. "He's almost too big for you to carry now," he said quietly.

"Never," she said, smiling through an irrational haze of moisture.

"Come on," he said, and walked up the stairs with Billy against his chest and a sack hanging from his arm. "I was worried about you," he said.

"Why?"

"I don't know. When you left last night I felt empty, incomplete." He was still holding Billy as he spoke.

"Did they bother you a lot?" he asked, and Peggy knew he meant his family.

"Grams is dear," she said. "The others . . . well, I don't think they like to clown around with clowns much." She smiled, then took Billy from his arms and took him off to bed. When she came back Mike was standing in the shadows over in the corner of the living room.

"What are you doing?"

"Trying to figure out how to work this thing." He was turning buttons on her record player, an ancient machine she'd picked up at a garage sale so she could play music for Billy.

"Why?"

"Because," he said slowly, "because I missed dancing with the most beautiful woman at the ball, and I want to make up for it."

Peggy frowned. She hadn't turned on any lights except for the small table lamp inside the door, and they were both standing in shadows. "What do you mean?"

"I mean my Cinderella escaped. But I've found her, and I've come to claim the dance I missed." The machine started to work then. Mike had put on one of the records he'd brought, soft, soothing, old-time band music, full of rhythm and beat. "I had to rummage through my father's old records," he said. "You'd be surprised how hard it is to find records. Everything is on tapes or CDs." When he turned back to her, music was filling the small room, rich instrumental music that was sentimental and romantic, filled with golden horns and smooth basses, saxophones bursting out in cool, pulsing melodies that made slipping into Mike's arms the most natural movement in the whole world.

He held her close, his hand on the small of her back and his head bent to breathe in the wonderful mix of aromas—her hair, her skin, her sensuality.

They didn't speak for a long time. Instead the music took over, and they moved as one, across the worn rug of her tiny living room, one long shadowy figure. Peggy felt the music inside her, controlling her heartbeat, her breathing. They had never danced together, not once. And they were a perfect pair, two creatures moving in dreamy acquiescence. Peggy had no sensation of turning or stepping, of moving her body.

They danced until all the records had been played and the room grew quiet with only the sound of their breathing breaking the silence. They stood there together, in the middle of the room, and Peggy kept her head tight against his chest, felt his hand on her back, his cheek rubbing gently against her hair.

He left a short while later, telling her he couldn't trust himself to stay longer. They had agreed days before not to be together for the night with Billy there, and Mike knew his resolve was strong but not superhuman. He stood at the door, holding her tight. "One of these days we need to touch the future."

Peggy nodded.

"But not tonight," he said. "You look like you could use some sleep."

She nodded again, tired and dreamy and hanging tightly on to the wonderful feeling of dancing through the night with Mike.

His low laughter tickled her cheek. He kissed her, and then he was gone, and Peggy knew without question she'd sleep better tonight.

THE NEXT DAY, while she and Joe and a few others were discussing some promo work for the documentary, Joe's secretary interrupted them to tell Peggy she had an important phone call.

In the lobby were dozens of balloons, a giant bouquet that filled the whole office, and a note that said, "To my clown, the love of my life."

"And he's on the phone, as well," said the secretary, as if Mike were somehow omnipresent.

"Oh," Peggy said with an apologetic smile.

"It's Mr. Kendrick," the secretary added.

Peggy smiled and took the call.

"Hi," Mike said. "Can't talk long but I would like to invite you to be my escort Friday night at the annual company dinner."

For a minute Peggy was silent. Then she said with forced brightness, "Company dinner?"

"Uh-huh. It's very festive. The board members come, stockholders, some important clients. Sometimes the governor comes. The mayor, you never know."

"The mayor...and me..."

"Sounds like a song."

"Friday?"

"Just wanted you to get it on your calendar so you have time to get a sitter."

Peggy was silent. An uncomfortable flutter disturbed her stomach. This felt oddly like a coming-out party. Peggy Shilling is introduced to society. She cringed. The last thing in the world she wanted to do was go to the Kendrick company dinner. But Mike wanted her there; he was saying something to her here, she knew, and she needed to respond.

"Peggy?" he said. "I really have to go. I have a meeting in a couple of minutes—"

"Of course, Mike," she said quickly. "I'd love to go."

His laughter rolled across the wires. "No, Peggy," he said. "Love isn't the operative word here, at least not in regard to company dinners. But thank you. I want you to be with me."

It helped a little that Joe would be there. Mike's mother would be there, of course, the sisters, and

Grams. Yes, Grams! As long as she could hang out with Grams, she'd be okay.

On his end, Mike hung up, grabbed his attaché case and headed to the meeting. *Great!* he thought. *She'll come. And everyone will know how I feel about this incredible woman. And Peggy will know, too. Mostly, Peggy will know.* He hadn't had much time to sort things through, and the idea for the dinner had come to him just minutes before he called her, but somehow it seemed a good idea.

He had come to a bunch of realizations this week. He knew he wanted Peggy with him; she brought love and laughter and a strange kind of significance into his life that hadn't been there before. He knew that when he wasn't with her he was wishing he was, and that the thought of Peggy being absent from his life was unbearable. What he didn't know were specifics, but he'd handled some of the most complicated business transactions in the entire country; certainly, together, he and Peggy could work out specifics.

THE REST OF THE WEEK was a blur for Peggy. She thanked God that she was busy; it kept her from calling Mike and telling him she had a horrid case of a very rare and extremely contagious South American disease. And then she thanked God for Casey, whose wonderful closet was as well stocked as Bloomingdale's. Casey pulled out a sapphire blue, off-the-shoulder dress that even Peggy had to admit made her look elegant.

And when Mike showed up at her door in his tuxedo, she truly felt like Cinderella with her handsome prince. She tried not to stare at Mike, but he was almost startlingly handsome in the elegant, tailored tux. "Oh, Mike, you look wonderful," she said in hushed tones.

Mike smiled slowly. "Me?" He stepped into the apartment and led Peggy by her hand over to better light. He held her at arm's length and looked at her carefully from the top of her thick auburn hair, brushed to a sheen tonight and hanging loosely about her bare shoulders, to the bottom of the flowing gown. She wore simple, dangling cut-glass earrings that hung low and caught the light, breaking it up into tiny stars and matching the dancing light in her green eyes. Mike swallowed hard. She seemed of another world, an ethereal, untouchable beauty, and for a minute he couldn't speak. Then he blinked once, focused back on her smile and said, "Peggy, I could stand naked next to you and no one would notice me tonight. You are so beautiful."

His voice was low, from deep in his throat, and the tone of it sent ripples of desire through Peggy. She touched his arm and said, "Mike, I don't think I should dwell on that thought too long. We'll never make it to the dinner." She took his arm and smiled tenderly at the man who had stolen her heart completely.

THE COMPANY DINNER was elegant and planned to perfection. It was held in a private club, a bastion for families like the Kendricks and as foreign to Peggy as Greek drachmas. But she remembered Mike's words, felt his hand on her arm, and was able to hold her head high as they walked together into the dark oak-paneled room.

Peggy held her smile as she was introduced to Chicago's wealthiest and finest. Mike's company vice presidents and their wives paraded by and shook her hand, faces she had glimpsed but not really seen at the charity ball spoke to her in lovely, well-modulated voices that held a touch of the east in their Midwestern tones.

It was the light in Mike's eyes, the warmth that flooded her when he looked at her that kept her going from group to group, smiling, laughing lightly.

By the time Mike's mother approached Peggy she was feeling more confident, more able to get through the hours left in the evening. Mike excused himself for a minute and left her in his mother's company.

"Peggy, you look lovely," Mrs. Kendrick said graciously and then she proceeded to introduce Peg to a handful of women, mostly board members' wives with golf-tan faces and dressed in elegant gowns. The talk was reserved but polite and Peggy listened while they discussed current art exhibits, daughters and granddaughters planning for the Christmas Ball and Passavant Cotillion, and the most recent garden party meeting.

It was almost time for dinner and Peggy looked around briefly for Mike, then tried to focus back on the conversation. She had nearly succeeded when a familiar voice traveled across the cocktail chatter. "Dr. Laugh A. Lot!" the voice said and the next minute a white-haired man appeared at Peggy's side.

Peggy looked up into the eyes of the director of the medical staff at Children's Hospital. "Hello, Dr. Harris," she said softly. The small group with which she was standing had grown silent as the doctor approached.

"I thought it was you," the doctor was saying, "but I couldn't be sure. Without your red wig and all that makeup it was difficult to tell." He laughed then, a convivial laugh intended to make Peggy smile.

She forced one to her lips.

"Makeup? Laugh a lot?" a woman in a beautiful beaded dress said.

Claire Kendrick turned toward the woman and said, "Peggy is involved in charity work at the hospital."

When she paused Dr. Harris boomed, "Peggy is a clown, and the best in the business!"

Peggy felt the red flush creeping up her chest, her neck, coating her cheeks. She lowered her eyes, tried to smile, tried to accept his compliment as graciously as if he had told her she had just won the Chicago Woman of the Year award.

Claire Kendrick's friends smiled politely. "A clown," one said. "How quaint."

The word bounced across Peggy's consciousness. Quaint...oh, lord. And then she prayed the lady wouldn't say more because she wasn't at all sure what she would say back. Her smile was wavering already.

"Say, Peggy," Dr. Harris went on, "I have great news for the clown troupe and you'll now be the first to know. Because of the success of the recent fundraisers we're going to be able to up the clown ante, so to speak. In essence, Dr. Laugh A. Lot, you have been given a raise.''

"The clowns are paid?'' Mrs. Kendrick asked.

"Sure, Claire,'' Dr. Harris said. "But not nearly enough. They do an incredible job.''

"I don't doubt that, Sheldon. I simply misunderstood.''

Peggy swore later she could *feel* the thoughts of the women standing around her, these charity leaders of the city. The realization that she—someone standing in their midst as one of *them*—was being paid for work that was close in kind to their volunteer activities was an embarrassment. She swallowed hard. And then she turned her brightest smile to Dr. Harris and said, "Thank you, Dr. Harris. That will be wonderful news to everyone!'' And with the brightness still in her voice, she turned slightly and spoke to the others. "We lost a couple of very fine clowns recently because they couldn't afford to continue. Several do this full-time. This will be a great help.''

"It is a job for all of you, then?'' asked the lady in the beaded dress.

"Yes.''

"I thought perhaps it was something intended to make the children feel better.''

"Oh, it's that and more, Betty,'' said Dr. Harris. "But that doesn't mean these people shouldn't get paid for it. I hope what *I* do makes the kids feel better, too. And I have to admit, my family doesn't mind a bit that I pick up a paycheck.'' He laughed again, that same resounding laugh, and Peggy would have

hugged him except it didn't seem the appropriate be-
havior just then.

"And yourself?" persisted the lady named Betty.
"Is this being a clown a full-time job for you, Peggy?"

Peggy swallowed hard, then said cheerfully, "No,
it doesn't work out for me to do it full-time, finan-
cially, that is. So I work at a couple of other jobs, as
well."

There, she thought. I am now naked. There is
nothing more for them to see. Unless she started talking about Billy, about the wonderful day she found
him in a basket on the doorstep.... The thought of it
all made her smile grow, and that was what Mike saw
as he walked up beside her.

"Hi," he said.

Peggy's smile grew as it focused on him. It was
Mike, her knight, her prince, come to rescue her. And
then, much to Peggy's relief, he slipped an arm around
her waist and announced to his mother that he was
stealing her away to introduce her to some others.
Little did he know, Peggy thought, that he didn't have
to steal her away at all; Claire Kendrick would have
gladly *given* her away.

The ride home was quiet. Peggy was exhausted,
having given every ounce of energy to the evening, to
smiling, to making appropriate responses. At the dinner R. J. Kendrick had announced that in six months
the reins of Kendrick Enterprises would change completely over to his son while he stayed on as chairman
of the board. Peggy had sat at the table in silence,
smiling up at Mike, listening to the applause and feeling a part of her being scooped out and sent off with

the empty dessert plates. And the hollow that remained was filled with dread. The announcement hadn't been a surprise; everyone had known Mike would eventually control the company. The only surprise was that it was this soon.

She looked over at Mike. His eyes were on the road. Every now and then, having felt her gaze, he looked over and smiled at her.

Mike walked up the three flights of stairs, his hand on the small of her back, and when they reached the top and he'd unlocked the door he took her in his arms and looked deep into her eyes, deep down into her soul.

Peggy felt her heart expand. She didn't want him to leave. She didn't think she could bear it if he left her tonight, left her with all the thoughts and fears that were taking root inside her, tiny seeds, ready to grow into full-blown worries. "Mike," she said, "Billy's across the hall tonight...at Carmen's...."

Swiftly, as if there was some unseen force compelling him to move, he lifted Peggy into his arms and, without turning on a light, carried her into the tiny bedroom.

And there, with the moon lighting their way, they urgently, poignantly, loved each other.

Chapter Thirteen

Peggy awoke out of a tangle of dreams. As her eyes adjusted to the hazy light of morning she saw Mike moving silently across the room. He had showered and was now gathering his clothes together. He looked over at her when she stirred and smiled softly. "Good morning, my love," he said, and moved to her side. He bent over, a hand placed on either side of her, and kissed her.

Peggy lay still, basking in the pleasure of it. But when he pulled away she frowned. "Mike?"

"I have to go, Peggy."

Peggy glanced at the clock. It was six o'clock. She looked back at Mike. "I don't like it when you leave, I don't like it when I leave you. Something opens up inside me and a cold breeze moves in."

Mike was buttoning his shirt. He paused, considering her words. "I know, Peg. I feel the same way."

"Does it scare you as much as it does me?"

"Scare might not be the word."

"I watched you last night, so at ease in that world of yours. And—" She paused. *And pulling me along behind* was what she had thought to say, but she held the words back, unable to toss all her doubts and fears right out there in front of them. Maybe if she played with them a little longer, picked at them, they would disappear. "Have you had coffee?" she asked, changing the subject.

"I'll get some later. Now I need to go home and change and then drive downtown to a meeting."

"On Saturday?"

"My father called it. Sometimes it's easier to get everyone together on Saturdays. And we needed to meet—some decisions need to be made."

"I understand. Go, and as my aunt Bessie used to say, 'May the wind be at your back.'" She sat up as she spoke so she could see him when he left, and the sheet fell to her waist.

Mike tossed his tuxedo jacket over one shoulder and sucked in a lungful of air. He strode over to her side, ran a finger along her jaw, down over the silky-smooth skin of her breast. And then he kissed her. He straightened up slowly and stood for a minute looking down at her. "You're a witch, Peggy, a beautiful, incredible, wonderful witch, and if I stay here one more minute I'll be lost."

He would be lost, he'd said. Peggy watched him disappear through the door and lay back against the pillows. And that was the irony of it all, she thought, because *she already was.*

ON SUNDAY PEGGY GAVE a bridal shower for Casey. The frantic activity was a blessing; it kept her worries at bay. She didn't have time to replay the scene with

Mike's mother at the dinner nor time to think about Mike's own presence that night, so powerful, so at ease in that power. And it was just the beginning.

She hadn't seen Mike since he had walked out her door the morning before, his stiff white shirt open haphazardly at the collar and a lover's smile easing the strong lines of his face. She had never seen him look more handsome.

The image stayed with her, through the day and the night, and now she brought it with her to Casey's but tried to keep it at a distance. She picked up a handful of ragged wrapping paper and tossed it into the garbage bag. "Two weeks, Casey, and you will have forsaken single womanhood forever!" Peggy said. "Can you believe it?" Most of the guests had left, and they were cleaning up the last remnants of the party.

"Two weeks...and, Peggy, you know what? I can't wait," Casey said.

"I know, Case. I can see that. It's right, you're ready, and the world is at your feet." Peggy sipped the last of her punch and carried the glass into the kitchen. Casey followed.

"I don't know as how I'd go that far, but this is right and good. I'm tired of having to schedule the intersecting of our lives. It simply doesn't make sense. I want to live with Pete, love him whenever I feel like it. I want to grow old together and buy matching rocking chairs."

Peggy laughed. "I think there's an excluded middle in there somewhere," she said, "but I get the gist."

Casey's happiness went home with Peggy, floating around in her mind, weaving in and out of her thoughts of Mike. But it wasn't a smooth merging; nothing was settling down into a feeling of *rightness* and Peggy found herself on the verge of tears for no reason whatsoever.

She needed Mike, needed to hear his voice to relieve the irrational anxiety eating away at her. With Billy on her lap, she called his house.

Stella answered and seemed happy to hear her voice. "He's out for the evening, Peggy. Dinner at his parents' home, I believe."

Peggy nibbled on her bottom lip. He hadn't invited her, but that was okay. Why should he? He knew things hadn't been smooth as silk between his mother and her at the company dinner. And there was no written law that said he had to take her home to dinner with him. Why was she acting this way? Peggy frowned, silently scolding herself.

"And my little friend Billy?" Stella was saying. "When is he going to come back to visit me again?"

"Soon, Stella," Peggy said, but the words sounded empty and she quickly ended the conversation and hung up.

MORNING CAME much too early and Peggy dragged herself out of bed. The day was another busy one. A meeting with Joe in the morning and a doctor's appointment for Billy in the afternoon. And Mike had mentioned last Friday taking her and Billy out for dinner, since Billy had missed the company bash. A busy day, a good day. She scooped a giggling Billy out of his crib and nuzzled his neck with her nose before standing him on the floor. Yes, the day was good. Life was good. And with renewed energy she pushed away all unsettling thoughts and followed Billy into the kitchen in search of bananas.

An hour later she was on the bus, heading toward the studio offices. She usually found someone to talk to, but today she wanted to sit alone, close her eyes and think about her life.

A headline on a discarded newspaper lying on the vacant seat next to hers wiped such lofty aims aside: Kendrick Plant In Chanooga Falls Lays Off Workers.

Peggy picked it up and her eyes scanned the double-columned article. Over two hundred workers had been laid off. A paper plant, it said. She frowned, thinking of the families involved, of her *own* family when William Shilling had been laid off after twenty-five years with the company. She rubbed her arms to ward off the chill. All those families—kids, wives, husbands—their lives turned upside down in a day's time. That's how it had been in her family. A normal day, turned into a nightmare. She could still remember her father coming home that night, remembered his attempt at lightness—it would be okay, maybe even better. But of course it never was.

When she arrived at the filming offices Joe was already there. Peggy walked in and sat down, ready to work.

"Peggy?" Joe looked at her curiously, his head leaning slightly to one side. "What's up? Where's the Peggy two-step, the famous Dr. Laugh A. Lot who rescued us from another dose of charity doldrums?"

Peggy managed a smile. "Glad you liked the show."

"I thought it was great. Here we work together every day and I didn't know you did that."

"Well, I do. And I love it."

"I could tell." He paused. He had overheard Nancy and some others at the company dinner talking about Peggy and her work as a clown. He could tell from the conversation they didn't know quite what to do with the information. It wouldn't have mattered to them at all, except that Peggy was at the dinner as Mike Kendrick's companion. And that mattered a lot.

Joe had stepped in, praising Peggy, talking about what an extraordinary person she was, but then afterward he had felt worse. He was justifying Peggy to them, he realized, and that was demeaning to her. She needed no justification. He wondered now if she had felt any of it, caught any of the vibes sent out from the people there, people who couldn't quite figure out why *Peggy* was there. But that wasn't something he could talk to her about. So instead he smiled and said, "You know, I was thinking maybe we could do a documentary on the clown troupe some day, give the group some exposure."

"That would be nice, Joe."

"But not nice enough to turn that frown into your usual cheery demeanor, huh?"

"Sorry. I was a little disturbed by this." She handed him the folded paper.

Joe glanced at the headline, then back to Peggy. "Yeah, it's a shame. That's the gruesome side of business, I guess."

"But does it have to be?"

"Sometimes it does, it seems."

"This time?"

"Peggy, you know as much about that as I do." He handed her a cup of coffee. "Now come on, kiddo, we've some work to do here."

"R.J. made the announcement, the paper says," she said, "but Mike was quoted, also."

"Mike hates stuff like this. I'm sure it wasn't easy for him to talk about it. But that's life."

"Is it?" Peggy felt the sting of tears but held them back. She thought of her mother, not getting out of bed for days, not knowing what to do after her father lost his job.

Joe looked at her for a long time. "Yes, Peggy, it is," he said finally. "And it's also a fact of life that we need to get to work ourselves, or this documentary is never going to see the light of day." He handed her a piece of paper. "Would you mind going to the library and checking out these statistics? I'd send someone else but there's no one available."

"I don't mind," Peggy said, and she took the paper and escaped out into the hot summer day, alone with her thoughts.

In the library she pulled the volumes that she needed off the shelf, and then, before she fully realized what she was doing, she found herself at the microfiche machine, reading every article she could find on the Chanooga Falls paper plant.

Hours later, when dark shadows fell across the wide oak table, Peggy, startled, looked up at the clock on the wall. It was nearly six o'clock. Frantic, she scooped up her papers, stuffed everything into her purse and hurried outside to find a taxi. It would dec- imate her budget, but she was two hours late.

When she reached her apartment, Carmen was as calm as always. Her big date for the evening, she claimed, was with a child psychology text and could certainly be put off. Billy threw his arms around his mother and dribbled on her shoulder.

"He's getting a new tooth," Carmen said proudly, as if she personally were responsible.

"Great. That's great."

"And finally," Carmen said, "you are to call Mike Kendrick as soon as you can." Her eyes lit up. "He called three times."

Peggy nodded, her thoughts flitting back to the newspaper articles. She knew what Casey would tell her: this wasn't any of her business, and she should let it alone. But she couldn't, she couldn't shake it off. And she couldn't get the two or three hundred fami- lies who now had zero income out of her mind.

As soon as Carmen left she dialed Mike's number.

"Darlin'," he said, "where've you been?"

"I was working on some things for Joe in the li- brary." There now, leave it alone, a small voice said. A louder one refused to let her. "And while I was there," she rushed on, "I read up a little on this Chanooga Falls plant that is laying off workers."

"You've read up on it? Why?"

"Because I was upset about it."

Mike was genuinely puzzled. "Why? I mean, it isn't even around here. Why would you be upset?"

"Because all those people, Mike, they're losing their jobs!"

"I know, Peggy. And it's crummy, but it happens. It had to be done."

"Because the company wasn't making any money."

"Yes, and other reasons."

"As best I can figure out, Michael—" She paused. It was the first time she had ever called him Michael. *Michael,* the Kendrick heir. And suddenly it stood for all the tiny fears and doubts clouding her love. "As best I can figure out," she went on, "that plant was purchased by Kendrick Enterprises for the sole purpose of shutting it down and selling its assets."

"We haven't done that—"

"Yet. But you plan to, don't you?"

There was silence on the other end of the phone.

"You are going to do that, aren't you?"

"Peggy, I love you. But I don't like being put on trial. You don't know half of the details about this transaction. You can't begin to understand it."

His voice sounded weary. Peggy bit down on her bottom lip. She felt the tears again.

"Peggy?" Mike tried to add lightness to his voice. "Peggy, are we having our first fight?"

Peggy smiled through her tears. "Yeah, I think we are."

"Over a paper plant in Chanooga Falls?"

"But, Mike—"

"Peggy," he interrupted, "I want to see you. I want the pleasure in person of making up from our first fight. So can we table the paper plant for now? We can talk about it in the office tomorrow morning when the sun is shining. But tonight, just for tonight, let's put it aside." His voice dropped, then grew husky, and he said, "I love you, Peggy. I wake up every day and there's something different in my life. I stop for a minute to figure it out, and that's it, that's what it is—it's my love for you."

Peggy's breath caught in her throat. She brushed the tears off her cheeks. "Yeah, Kendrick. I know."

"And?"

"And I love you, too. So very, very much."

BUT THE NEXT DAY as Peggy headed in to the office, the sun wasn't shining and the weatherman was predicting rain. Peggy wondered if it was an omen.

The night before she and Mike had taken Billy to a restaurant that sent the hamburgers and French fries to each table via a little electric train, and Billy loved it. Then Mike had suggested going to a nearby park and Peggy had found herself watching him push Billy on the merry-go-round and thinking about what an incredible father he'd make. And by the time Billy had been tucked in and they were relaxing on the couch in one another's arms, the fight was well patched up, and for a while, at least, she had forgotten all about the myriad fears that were growing vines around her heart.

She checked her watch now and saw that she had an hour before she was to meet with Joe. She had time to see Mike at his office, time for him to alleviate her fears and explain the whole mess about the paper plant in terms she could understand. And everything would be okay.

"Peggy!" Mike said when she appeared at his office. It was early and even Mike's secretary hadn't come in yet. Mike closed the door behind her and took her in his arms. "What a terrific way to start the day."

Peggy pulled away. She'd never get a single question out if Mike was touching her because every time he did, her mind turned to mush. Or lust, as Casey put it. She smiled brightly. "I came to talk about the paper plant."

"Paper plant?"

"Chanooga Falls."

"Oh, sure, *that* paper plant. Sure, Peggy, I forgot."

She glanced out the window. "Except it isn't sunny like you promised."

"No, I guess not." Mike leaned back against the desk and folded his arms. "Okay, Peggy, what do you want to know?" Mike held back the irritation that surfaced. His business was in a private realm, something he didn't discuss with anyone except those involved. But he knew Peggy was only trying to understand, and he *had* told her they'd talk about it, so he owed her that much.

"I don't understand how Kendrick Enterprises can justify doing this," Peggy said. "The plant was purchased just a short while ago, and the news articles stated it would benefit the town because Kendrick could put money into the company, and therefore the town."

"They always say that, Peg. It's standard press release stuff. We weren't positive at the time *what* we were going to do with it. We had a couple of options."

"And you chose the one that would throw hundreds of families into chaos? Maybe even destroy them?"

Mike frowned. "That's a little strong, Peggy. These people will get other jobs. Trust me."

"Will they? Are you sure? Or will the men trudge home day after day, disheartened, depressed, demoralized...." Her eyes were blazing now.

Mike looked at her for a minute without speaking. Something was going on here that went beyond his understanding, beyond the situation.

At that moment there was a single firm knock on the door, and R. J. Kendrick walked in.

"Michael, I had hoped you'd be in," he said. And then he spotted Peggy, her face flushed, her hands curled into small fists.

"Oh, Miss Shilling," he said with a nod in her direction. "I'm sorry. I assumed Michael was alone."

He stood there then, waiting for Peggy to leave. Instead, she turned toward him. "Mr. Kendrick, I came in to talk with Mike about the Chanooga Falls plant, but perhaps you'd be able to help me understand the situation."

Mike looked at her. " Peggy, I don't think—"

"It will only take a moment," she said, her eyes still on Mr. Kendrick. "I only want you to explain why you're doing it."

R. J. Kendrick's thick white brows pulled together and deep furrows formed where they almost touched. "Why, young lady, would I do that?"

"Because it doesn't make sense. Because hundreds of families will be thrown into confusion and hardship. Because you don't *need* to do it."

"I don't quite see how our company *needs* are your concern, Miss Shilling." His mouth was tight, his jaw set.

Peggy looked down for a brief moment, then met his eyes again. "I know I'm appearing impudent and presumptuous, Mr. Kendrick, but maybe someone needs to bring it to your attention." She could feel her heart pounding, could feel good sense leave her in a mass exodus. "Maybe someone needs to jar your conscience!"

"Peggy, let's drop it," Mike cut in. "I need to talk to my father. I'll talk with you later." He held his voice steady, hoping Peggy would read his message. He was damn mad she had spoken out that way, stepped into an area that really didn't concern her. But anger aside, he didn't want her hit by the force of his father's anger; instinctively he wanted to protect her.

Peggy stood silently. She looked from one man to the other, and then she slowly picked up her purse from the floor and walked out of the office.

PEGGY NEVER MADE IT to her meeting with Joe.

Instead, she caught a bus at the corner and rode it to the beach. The angry gray clouds that hung over the lake had sent sunbathers and swimmers home, and a lone golden retriever, his long hair waving like wheat in the crisp breeze, ran in and out of the waves.

Peggy slipped out of her shoes and left them on the pathway, then walked down to the shore. Her feet dug into the wet sand and soon the tide covered them, all the way up to her ankles. And then she cried, long mournful cries that came from deep down inside her and were caught up and tossed about by the waves.

The dog, alerted by her cries, turned and ran to her side. His long nose, speckled with sand, nudged her hand, and Peggy absently patted his head. "Oh, pup," she said, "why is life so difficult?"

The dog shook his wet fur in reply and splattered Peggy with water. She smiled sadly. "I wish I could do that, shake it all off—" And then the tears came again, stronger this time, and Peggy didn't try to stop them. Days of bottled-up emotion poured out of her. She had been fooling herself, playing Cinderella games, pretending that there was a life with Mike... and it was so foolish. Peggy's folly, she thought, that's what all this is. She wiped the tears from her cheeks and began to walk along the shore, the dog at her side, her eyes scanning the rough sea for answers.

She must have known the truth days ago, weeks, maybe, but she had refused to see it. Hadn't even Casey warned her? Her relationship with Mike was a fantasy, a Cinderella dream, and it would never be able to bear up beneath the burden of reality. But she loved him so, that was the agony of it. Loved him with her whole heart and soul. But they were star-crossed lovers, or whatever it was the songs and books immortalized. And finally, today, in the heat of her anger, she realized the truth of it all.

It didn't have much to do at all with Kendrick Enterprises, she knew. That was simply a vehicle for releasing the hidden fears. No, it wasn't a company or a plant closing or unemployed people. It was her...and it was Mike. Two people who should never have let themselves fall in love.

IT WAS LATE when she returned that night. The rain had finally come and driven Peggy from the shore, and as she walked along the wet pavement from the bus stop, it started again. She looked up into the gray mounds of clouds and let the raindrops run down her cheeks, her forehead, into her mouth. Small rivers ran down onto her shoulders, and her hair was slippery and collected in wet strands that stuck to her cheeks. She stopped at the corner across from her apartment and let the rain pummel her. And this time when the tears started again, they were washed away by the rivers of rain.

When she walked into the apartment Carmen and Maxie were both there, Carmen standing near the door with a towel in her hand. She immediately began to dry Peggy's hair.

"I'm okay, guys, really."

"Okay, my foot!" cried Maxie. "We watched you from the window, standing there, sobbing. What's the matter?"

Peggy stood in the tiny foyer. Small puddles of water collected around her. She looked down the hall and saw that Billy was asleep in his crib. She bit down on her bottom lip, tried to hold back the torrent that pressed angrily against her eyelids.

"Mike," Carmen said.

Peggy nodded.

"What happened?"

Peggy's voice was blocked by her tears and her great sadness. She slipped out of her shoes, walked over and curled up on the end of the couch.

Maxie and Carmen stood there, unsure of what to do. Peggy shook her head. "I think...I think I should be alone for a while." She looked up, a look of apology swimming in her tears.

"Okay," Carmen said. "But I'll check in." She hugged her and she and Maxie quietly left, closing the door behind them.

Peggy closed her eyes. But that was a mistake. Behind her lids, all across the panorama of her mind, was Mike. Her Mike, the best man she had ever met...the one at last that made her heart pound and her whole self light up. The one that made the voice say, *This is it, this is the man for Peggy!* But he wasn't the man for Peggy. The voices were wrong. Horribly, painfully wrong. Peggy reached for the box of tissues, and mercifully, before the last was used, she fell asleep.

Waking was painful. Her head was throbbing and for a moment she thought the shrill noise was inside her head. Finally the fog lifted and she fumbled for the phone.

Mike's voice was far away. "Peggy," he said, "I need to talk to you."

She started to say no. And then the unfairness of that swept through her with a new pain, the pain of seeing Mike, of loving Mike and of saying goodbye.

"I'll cancel my appointments. I'll come over."

Her mind struggled to figure out the least painful way to handle this. Finally she spoke, her voice hollow. "No, don't do that, Mike. I'll meet you somewhere."

"My place?"

"No," she said quickly. Finally they decided to meet at noon in the small park near Mike's office where they had often met for lunch. Peggy would have preferred a bus station or a busy street corner, someplace that held no memories, but at Mike's suggestion, she settled on the park.

Carmen showed up before Peggy had a chance to call her. "I want to help, Peg," she said, her eyes showing how much she cared. Peggy hugged her. "Thanks, Carmen. I know you do. And you are helping, by taking Billy today. I don't want him to see me so sad. It will upset him."

From the look on her face, Carmen was upset, too, Peggy could see, but she couldn't talk about it with anyone, not until she saw Mike, and maybe not ever.

Mike was waiting when she got there. He looked awful, Peggy thought, and then she touched a finger to her puffy eyes and knew she wasn't a magazine cover girl herself. "Hi, Mike," she said.

Mike didn't touch her. Instead he shoved his hands into his pockets and looked at her with great longing. "This is about more than the company business, isn't it?"

"It's not about the company business at all, Mike, at least not directly." She'd practiced this on the bus. Don't get too close, keep your voice strong, don't, above all, *don't* touch him.

But it was far easier on the bus when all she had to look at was the cracked plastic of the seat in front of her. She tried not to focus on his eyes, and started in again. "It's us, Mike, you and me."

"I love you, Peggy," he said softly.

"No! Don't do that, Mike." She held her hands in front of her frantically.

Her eyes were huge, round and luminous, and Mike thought he could see all the way down into her soul through them. And the soul he saw was tortured. Peggy was leaving him. She was going to turn and walk out of his life. "But I do love you, Peggy," he said. "And if we're going to talk about anything, we need to be honest, and that is the most basic truth ruling my life right now. I love you. In spite of all the differences between us, I love you."

"And?" she said, her chin lifting and her eyes glazing with tears. "See, Mike, that's the problem, there's no *and*. We love each other but there's no *and*. No happy ever after. That whole thing about the plant . . . it was simply a catalyst. It broke the dam, I guess, and all the uncertainties I've felt about us came tumbling out. Our differences would destroy us eventually, Mike." She ached from the effort to hold back the tears.

Mike took a step toward her. "Peggy, I don't think you're giving us enough credit. *Me* enough credit. I love my family, but I'm not them. I—"

"It's not your family, Mike. It's not the fact that they don't like me. It's more than that, it's everything. Our frame of reference is all different. Our lives are different. And if we married, we would probably try to change each other.'' She shook her head and the slight movement caused tears to stream down her face.

''Peg, there's nothing I want to change about you. I love you the way you are.''

''You love me the way I am when we arrange things, surround ourselves with things that protect us . . . like Paradise Lake, and my apartment. But throw in a company dinner or charity ball, and it all gets tossed to hell. And we can't stay in our cocoon all our lives, Mike. I won't raise Billy that way. I can't. I can't throw him into an environment that's foreign to him, foreign to *me*. It's the square pegs and round hole thing, Mike. It breaks my heart . . . but I don't think I could build a life with you, with all that. I'd make you miserable, always contradicting, being the odd one out.''

Mike felt a growing fear inside himself. He took her by the hand and pulled her down onto a park bench. Then he held her shoulders and forced her to look at him. ''Peggy, I think you're blowing something out of proportion. Maybe you're not giving me enough credit. Do you think I care about appearances? About what others think? About—''

''Mike, you *have* to care! You're going to be running one of the most powerful businesses in Chicago. Of course it matters. I mean, who knows, they'll probably want you to run for mayor someday. I can't be a corporate wife, I can't keep my mouth shut when I should, but maybe the thing I can't do the most is be dependent on you, Mike.'' The tears started to fall when she said his name, the name she loved because it stood for the person who filled her with the greatest joy of her life.

"Peggy, you're being irrational."

She shook her head so vehemently that her hair stung her cheeks as it slapped against the skin. "No, Mike. I was irrational when I let myself fall in love with you. But these things are real. I'm real, the way I am—walking a picket line, dressing up like a clown or lord knows what. And I can't give that up, Mike, because if I did I'd shrivel up inside and then there would be nothing left there for you to love. Nothing."

She was crying now, heavy, copious tears that ran down her face and onto her lap. But she couldn't stop. The dam had burst.

"Peggy—" Mike started, but she stopped him by reaching out and covering his lips with the tips of her fingers. And then she stood, and before she threw her arms around him she turned and fled across the park.

Mike stood there for a long time, watching her until she was a speck on the horizon. And then he wiped the moisture from his eyes with the back of his hand and walked slowly back toward the glass-fronted sky-scraper that housed Kendrick Enterprises.

Chapter Fourteen

Peggy wandered around her apartment the next evening. Carmen had taken Billy to the park again and the emptiness was overwhelming. It was so quiet, such an enormous quiet. She couldn't have imagined the enormity of the pain she would feel without Mike. Would she have ended it if she had?

She shook her head and the slight movement started the tears again. She would have...yes, because she did it for Mike as well as for herself and Billy. Mike didn't fit in her life and he never would. And she didn't fit in his.

And that was the plain awful truth of it.

But if it was so right, why was she feeling so wrong? Why was her heart squeezed painfully; why did she feel that the world had been doused with buckets of awful gray paint and the sun would never ever shine through it again?

She passed a mirror and shuddered at her red puffy face. She could go to work at the hospital and she wouldn't even need makeup. Except she would frighten the kids, not comfort them and make them laugh. She frightened herself.

She had gone in to work that day, although it took every ounce of energy. Joe had held her, told her she looked like hell but Mike looked even worse. "Oh, Joe," she had said, her eyes wet, "why couldn't you and I have fallen in love? It would have been a much better match. At least we came from the same soil."

A tear wandered down her cheek and Joe caught it with the tip of his finger. "No one comes from the same soil, Pegs. Not really. You dig in wherever you are, it seems to me."

She thought of his words now as she wandered into the bedroom. They were nice words, but not practical. She spotted the last box of tissues in the middle of her bed. Slowly Peggy lowered her aching body down beside the box and, pulling the tissues out one by one, she cried herself to sleep.

When Carmen returned with Billy she bathed him and put him to bed, pulled a blanket up over Peggy and then curled up herself in the large chair beside the air conditioner in case either of her friends should need her during the night.

The next day Maxie came over with a sack of doughnuts.

"Maxie," Peggy said slowly, "could you stay with Billy? Carmen has class. I think I'm going home."

"Home?"

"To Gary. To see your mom. Just for a few hours. I'll be back, then. Casey's rehearsal dinner is tonight."

Maxie looked at her for a long time. "I guess you should do what you need to do," she said at last.

When Mike showed up on the third-floor landing three hours later, Maxie didn't even show surprise. He looked terrible. She took his arm and pulled him into Peggy's apartment. "You'd better come in, Mike. I'm afraid if anyone sees you they'll call the police."

Mike managed a thin smile. "Thanks, Maxie. I don't feel too terrific, either."

"Well, neither does Peggy, if that helps."

"She's not here, I guess."

"No." Maxie paused for a moment. And then she walked over to the table and scribbled down her mother's address, and without any regrets she handed it to Mike Kendrick.

IT TOOK LESS THAN two hours for Mike to get to Gary and find the small frame house on the edge of town. A squat woman with sparkling green eyes that danced just like Peggy's answered the door. She squinted for a minute, then smiled and before Mike could say anything she opened the screen door and told him to come inside. "You're Peggy's Mike," she said, not asking, simply nodding to herself, confirming it. "I'm her aunt Bessie."

"Is Peggy here?"

"No, Mike, she's not. She left a little bit ago. She went by the cemetery to visit her parents' graves."

Mike's face fell. He looked at Bessie and forced a smile. "I seem to be striking out."

"Come in and have some lemonade," Bessie said. "Then go back to Chicago and find that girl and marry her."

Mike was startled for a minute. And then he gave a short laugh. "Bessie, there is nothing I want more in this life than to marry your niece, but I have to tell you, she's not making it easy. And the damnable thing is, she left me wondering if maybe she wasn't right. If maybe this was too big for us. . . ."

"How long did you feel that way, young man?"

"About five minutes."

"Good!" Bessie said, then led him into the living room and got him some lemonade.

Mike looked around the small room. The walls and coffee table and shelves were filled with pictures in ornate frames. Bessie saw him looking and smiled. "This is how I keep my family around me." She picked up one and handed it to Mike. "Here are Peggy's mother and father in happier years."

Mike looked down at a handsome couple holding a beautiful toddler about Billy's age. Even then, Peggy's auburn waves and brilliant smile controlled the scene. The family was standing in front of a house that looked a lot like Bessie's.

"Peggy's father, William, my brother, worked for the Sanderson Manufacturing plant. He was a foreman and did a fine job. He loved Peggy and her mother fiercely. And he loved being in charge. He was in charge of everything, made everything right for the family. As you can see from the picture, Peggy's parents were older, nearly forty when Peggy was born. Sandra, Peggy's mother, was a lovely woman but very dependent on William. It used to worry me and I would try to entice her into a part-time job, but William wouldn't hear of it and Sandra didn't think she could handle it, so it never happened. When Peggy was almost a teenager William was laid off. Just like that, bingo, gone! It nearly destroyed him. He couldn't get another job except for part-time things here and there. His spirit was destroyed. He died a year later in a car accident. He was coming home from a job interview and someone ran a stop sign. And after that things got worse. Sandra couldn't function and Peggy was literally the head of the family. We all pitched in and helped, of course. When Sandra died a few years later, no one was surprised.''

Mike felt a pain slice through him as pieces of the puzzle began to fall into place.

"Mike, she's a complicated one, this woman you've chosen to love. She's strong and opinionated and every inch her own person. She wants Billy to grow up that way, too, and she's scared. Scared she'll lose control, scared that differences will be insurmountable and will consume her... or Billy...."

Mike stood. He nodded. "I love her, Bessie. She makes me a better person, and I'm good for her, too, whether she knows it or not. And I'm good for Billy. Peggy is so overwhelmed by the differences that she's failed to look at the things we have in common, the things that make us love one another."

"Well, then, you'll just have to show her, won't you?" Bessie stood beside the tall man and looked up at him. "So for heaven's sake, go and do it. She's a mess, that one. Never in all my years have I seen anyone so in love."

Before leaving, Mike drove through the neighborhood and tried to imagine a ten-year-old Peggy running along the uneven sidewalks, a sixteen-year-old Peggy coming home from a first date, a headstrong Peggy trying to hold a family together. And then he drove swiftly back to the city and for the first time in the longest hours of his life, he breathed deeply and felt good.

It was dark when he got back, and as he pulled into his driveway he realized there were a few things he had to do. Without a pause he put the car into reverse and drove off into the night.

THE WEDDING was beautiful and simple. Peggy watched her best friend as she promised to live her life together with Pete, to help him through all of life's happenings, and then they promised, together, to try to make the world a better, more peaceful, more loving place. Peggy smiled through her tears and watched Pete as he stood beside Casey, beaming, his handsome face alive with love.

Casey turned toward Peggy to get her bouquet. She took it from Peggy's hand, then leaned over and kissed her friend on the cheek. "This is what it's about, Peggy," she whispered. "I love you, and I don't want what I have to get away from you. Don't let it." And she smiled at Peggy, wiped a tear from her friend's cheek and turned back to join her husband as they prepared to walk back down the aisle as man and wife.

Peggy didn't think she could feel any more emotion. She thought she was drained, empty. But it came in waves, swooping down on her, lifting her up and crashing her against the edge of the shore. She had managed to get through the rehearsal dinner the night before but not without Casey pulling her into the women's rest room and giving her hell.

"You've never been a quitter, Peggy!" she had intoned. "Why now? Why are you giving up when Mike Kendrick is the best thing that ever came your way! Hell with differences and family name and a stuffy mother. People come around, Peggy! And even if they don't, you and Mike have enough without all that. And Billy...Billy would have two parents who thought he hung the moon. But the love...that may not come around again, Pegs."

All night long Peggy had thought about Casey's words. She was right, of course. A love like Mike's would never come around again because there would never be another love like this. And the strength of it seemed to have grown even stronger since she'd said goodbye to him, seemed to have even more control over her now than when they were together. She wondered vaguely if it would always be like that, if her life would be controlled by love for a man she couldn't have.

No, that was an inconceivable scenario, and by the time Peggy got home there was a flicker of hope lighting her heart. But Mike hadn't called, and when she gathered up all her courage and called his house, there was no answer.

She slept in bits and pieces, and by dawn she knew this wasn't going to work. No differences, no obstacle could possibly be greater than being without Mike altogether. No. It simply couldn't be.

She had made Mike angry, had made strong, emotional statements. Maybe it was no longer up to her. Mike had listened to what she'd said; perhaps he agreed. Maybe he was relieved that the problems were gone.

She looked up and saw Pete's best man looking at her. In the background she heard the swell of the organ. It was over. Quickly Peggy pulled herself from her thoughts and joined him to follow Pete and Casey back down the aisle.

In the back of the chapel, Mike stood behind the ushers, his eyes on Casey and Pete. He had been late, missed the ceremony. But the swelling recessional began as he slipped into the cool shadows at the back of the chapel. Casey looked beautiful. A perfect bride. And then she leaned over slightly to pat the cheek of an elderly woman sitting at the end of an aisle, and beyond her Mike spotted the reason he had come, the one woman, if she would have him, whom he would cherish all his life.

His heart stopped beating for a second, then began again, rapidly, pumping blood in a heady rush through his whole body. Peggy. *His beautiful Peggy,* walking down the aisle in a dress the color of crushed roses. His look was so powerful that he knew she would glance at him, and she did. Their eyes met and locked so powerfully together he wondered why others didn't notice the collision.

Peggy's eyes widened, damp with tears, filled with hope. Her heart gave a great leap and the light began to dance again in her eyes.

Silent words passed between them, carried along on a direct current, and by the time Peggy reached the end of the aisle Mike was there, his arms open, and she melted into them.

This might be a dream, she thought, pressing her cheek against his chest, wanting to feel his heartbeat, to become part of him. But if it was a dream she didn't want to wake up. She didn't want to ever be without Mike again.

"These have been the longest days of my life," she said, slowly tilting her head back to see his face.

Mike looked down at his watch, then back into her eyes. "Seventy-two hours and counting," he said.

Peggy wrapped her arms around his waist and walked with him out the side door, away from the crowd. Neither of them spoke for a long while. Instead they stood with their arms wrapped around each other, their hearts full.

"Peggy," Mike finally began, "I went to see my parents last night."

Peggy's head began to nod against his chest. "I know, Mike, I know how they feel about me, I know how angry I made your father—"

Mike didn't stop. It was as if she hadn't even spoken. "And I told them I was going to beg you to marry me. I told them you were the best thing that had ever happened to me, that you had brought a joy and peace and satisfaction to my life, that I would be a crazy fool to let you get away and I was going to fight like crazy so that you wouldn't."

"What did they say?" Her voice shook slightly as she asked. She knew what they would say; she knew they thought Peggy would be a horrible noose around their only son's neck.

"My father said, 'You have nothing in common.'"

Her voice was hushed. "Yes. And that's at the heart of it, Mike. He's right. We—"

Again Mike went on, his eyes never leaving her face. "And I said, 'No, Dad, you're dead wrong about that. We have so much in common that to let it go would be to pass up the best merger of all time. We both want desperately to be a family, we want to bring some joy into each other's lives, we both care about kids, we both love Billy and we'd even like to bring a few brothers and sisters into the world for him. Okay, so I presumed a little there. We can talk about it," he said, then went on. "I told him we share a passion for life, a desire to make the world a better place. We love Paradise Lake and the blue skies. And he finally stopped me because he could see I was going to go on for a long time."

"And your mother?" She could barely speak and the words wobbled as they passed between them.

"She approved in her own way."

"Which was?"

"She said, 'Well, dear, you can say goodbye to the Fairway Country Club but the Shorelane might consider you.'"

"Oh, Mike," she said. She laughed softly as her tears soaked into his white shirt. "You're sure we can do this?"

He nodded. "No doubts whatsoever. I'm not saying I'm not scared. I'll want to protect you sometimes from the snobbery and narrow-mindedness of people I'm associated with—and I won't be able to. I won't be able to change that."

"That doesn't bother me, Mike. Not if you love me, not if you're there. I feel the same about protecting *you*."

Mike laughed. "Grams wants to dance at our wedding. She said you were the best thing to happen to the Kendricks since she agreed to marry my grandfather and if you turn me down she will have lost a good deal of respect for me."

"That would be awful."

He pressed his nose into her hair and breathed in the familiar smell. "Yes . . ." he said.

"I love you, Mike Kendrick," Peggy said. She didn't want to cry again, but the tears stung painfully against her lids.

"There's one more thing," he said. His voice was husky. "I missed most of Casey's wedding because my father insisted on meeting with me this morning. I thought at first he had come up with new objections, and decided to meet it head-on, get it over with."

There was a catch in his voice, and Peggy looked up to see moisture in his eyes. "What was it, Mike?" Her heart stopped.

"It was this," he said, and he pulled from his pocket a packet of white legal-looking papers.

Peggy took them and unfolded them slowly. She didn't want to read them, didn't want anything to mar the joy or to tarnish the happiness that filled her. She read slowly and hesitatingly. And then she began to understand and she looked up at Mike, her heart so full it pained her.

"You got to the old man, Peggy. There's a soft spot there, and it seems to be for you. He said no one had ever talked to him the way you had, and although he didn't necessarily like it, he respected it. And maybe in time he would learn to like it. So he wanted you to have this as a wedding present."

Peggy looked down again at the papers. It was the deed to all the acreage around Paradise Lake. The hills, the stables and the lakeshore. "Oh, Mike. Your fishing spot...."

"*Our* fishing spot. Dad said he remembered spending time there with me and thought it would be a good spot for us to take 'the boy,' as he called him. When I reminded him that Billy would be his grandson, he looked up at me and said, 'Yes, and I know a damn sight more about fishing than you do. Maybe I'll use some of this damn semiretirement to teach him the fine points.'"

This time, Mike lifted Peggy's chin before the tears started to fall, and when they came they glistened like tiny jewels on her cheeks.

His eyes locked into hers. "Does all this mean a yes?"

But the question didn't require words for an answer. They both knew that, so Mike lowered his head and covered her single word with a kiss that spoke far more eloquently.

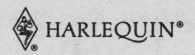

♦ HARLEQUIN®

THE TAGGARTS OF TEXAS!

Harlequin's Ruth Jean Dale brings you
THE TAGGARTS OF TEXAS!

Those Taggart men—strong, sexy and hard to resist...

You've met Jesse James Taggart in FIREWORKS!
Harlequin Romance #3205 (July 1992)

And Trey Smith—he's THE RED-BLOODED YANKEE!
Harlequin Temptation #413 (October 1992)

And the unforgettable Daniel Boone Taggart in SHOWDOWN!
Harlequin Romance #3242 (January 1993)

Now meet Boone Smith and the Taggarts who started it all—
in LEGEND!
Harlequin Historical #168 (April 1993)

Read all the Taggart romances!
Meet all the Taggart men!

Available wherever Harlequin Books are sold.

HARLEQUIN ◆ PRESENTS®

A Year
DOWN UNDER

In 1993, Harlequin Presents celebrates the land down under. In May, let us take you to Auckland, New Zealand, in SECRET ADMIRER by Susan Napier, Harlequin Presents #1554.

Scott Gregory is ready to make his move. He's realized Grace is a novice at business *and* emotionally vulnerable—a young widow struggling to save her late husband's company. But Grace is a fighter. She's taking business courses and she's determined not to forget Scott's reputation as a womanizer. Even if it means adding another battle to the war—a fight against her growing attraction to the handsome New Zealander!

Share the adventure—and the romance—of A Year Down Under!

Available this month in
A YEAR DOWN UNDER

A DANGEROUS LOVER
by Lindsay Armstrong
Harlequin Presents #1546
Wherever Harlequin books are sold.

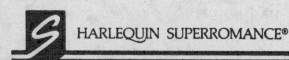
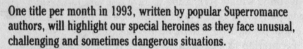